Red-Eye Ghost

by
Micky MacPhee

Illustrated by Jodie Cresswell

A *Moving On* Series Book

This book has been funded by
the Esmee Fairbairn Foundation,
the Tudor Trust and
Derbyshire Gypsy Liaison Group

Publisher Robert Dawson/Derbyshire
Gypsy Liaison Group
2004

Publisher Robert Dawson,
on behalf of Derbyshire Gypsy Liaison Group
188 Alfreton Road, Blackwell, Alfreton, Derbys DE55 5JH

ISBN 1-903418-50-X

The rights of Micky MacPhee to be identified as the author, and Jodie Cresswell the illustrator, of this work, has been asserted in accordance with the Copyright Designs and Patents Act 1988. All rights reserved. Other than for normal review purposes, no part of this publication may be reproduced, transmitted or stored in a retrieval system, in any form by any means, without permission in writing through the Publisher.

RA 9-14, CA 10y 8m

Printed by 4 Sheets Design and Print,
197 Mansfield Road, Nottingham, NG1 3FS

Red-Eye Ghost

MOVING ON series

Acknowledgement

Derbyshire Gypsy Liaison Group acknowledges with gratitude funding assistance given by the Esmee Fairbairn Foundation and by the Tudor Trust without whom these books would not have been possible.

This book is based on several requests from Scottish and English Traveller Education Services. We are grateful for their requests.

This book is intended as a stand-alone book for fairly proficient readers.

The *Moving On* Series
100+ Culture-specific books
for Traveller children

Pre-school/Toddler
4 planned

Key Stage 1
Houses and Homes

Key Stage 1 and 2
When Little Monsters Come to Call
Finches
*Dogs**
*Holiday bus**

Key Stage 2
How Rabbits Arrived in England
The Christening
*Wagons**
*Travel**
*Boxing**
*Old Crafts**
*The Rainbow Has No End**
*3 Mullo stories**
*Traveller Horses**
Red-Eye Ghost

**In preparation*

Key Stage 3
Hell and Damp Nation
Red-Eye Ghost

Available from DGLG, Ernest Bailey Community Centre, New Street, Matlock, Derbys. DE4 3FE OR Publisher.

Chapter 1

The little procession neared the top of the hillock.

"One last wee push!"

Johnny heard Granda's breath coming in short gasps as he heaved on the shafts at the front of the handcart. Behind, Johnny gritted his teeth and gave it every last bit of strength. Beside him, Granny had at last put away the foul smelling stumpy pipe she always smoked. She was alternately pushing and encouraging his younger sister Cathy and little brother Ewen.

Granda's old lurcher dog, Riley, followed wearily behind them all.

Slowly, the cart, laden high with the hazel wands and canvas, the pots and pans and blankets of every day life, reached the top of the small hill.

"Now hold it back a wee while!" Granda ordered as it set off down the far side.

At last, they were back on level ground. Beside him, Johnny heard the sea chattering onto the pebbled shore. He was ready to drop. They'd only walked three or four miles alongside the Galloway shore, but it was hard walking along a path made by sheep and not meant for a hand cart. Every here and there, they'd scaled one of the odd hillocks, over which the winding path led.

"Why are they here?" Johnny had asked Granda once.

Granda had looked grim. "Aakhh! They're the stones of ruined cottages. Where people once abided. Till they were driven away by the Great Sheep."

Johnny imagined a huge woolly animal, somehow pushing people from their homes. Granda saw him puzzling. "The owners of the land — they made the people leave so they could keep sheep here instead and make lots o' money." He nodded towards a flock of sheep on a hillside near one of the tumps. "Then they burned the houses so they couldnae come back."

Johnny shuddered. It seemed awfully cruel. He was glad they had a tent to stay in, even if was home made.

Ahead, another tump caused by the ruins of a house, the grass grown over, stood in their way. He dreaded the effort. "One last heave up here," Granda said.

"Another!" Ewen moaned.

"Aakhh, this really is the last time," Grandad gasped, heaving at the cart's shafts.

Johnny wedged his feet against a lump of stone, put his shoulder against the back of the cart, and heaved with all his strength, too. Beside him, Cathy and Gran were using every last ounce of their strength. Ewen pushed Johnny.

Then Granda said, "This'll do us. This is the place." You could almost hear everyone's sigh of relief.

"I knew it would be," Cathy called. She *always* knew, even when she didn't.

Something about it made Johnny realise that, somehow, Granda was right. This was the correct place to be, though he could never have explained why. It was beside the shore and there was plenty of driftwood. The mound and the Rowan trees gave some privacy and shelter from the offshore wind. Even though it was Spring, that West Scotland wind still had icy fingers to it. But there was something else. A sort of feel, that they were *meant* to be here, like that you get when you suddenly realise you've been somewhere before, but you know you haven't really. Kind of spooky.

"We'll pitch the bender here," Granda said. "We're doing this the proper ole way, like our people have 2000 years, since Christ hisself. Ewen, you fetch wood for the fire. Cathy, water from the burn."

"I was just going," she claimed.

Granda ignored her. "And you, Johnny laddie, help me with the tent while yer Gran unpacks yon hand cart."

As his sister and brother scuttled to get things ready, Johnny picked up the bent iron bar from which the kettle would soon hang over the fire.

"That's it," said Granda, throwing a heap of hazel wands off the cart. "Make holes with the saster."

"Aye, I know," Johnny insisted. He'd seen Granda put the old bender up often enough in the field near the caravan site where they usually lived. It was a summer treat for the kids to sleep out in it, like the old days of the Travelling People.

Johnny stabbed the pointed end of the saster into the thin turf to make a line of holes. Granda followed behind, pushing each wand into a hole as far as he could.

"Ackh, you great noodle, laddie! That's not deep enough."

He snatched the saster from Johnny and began to demonstrate. Then, like Johnny had already found, discovered that the stones were too near the surface to get down far. "Too stony. Never mind, we'll manage," he said. "Put your last hole just by the mound." He gave the kettle iron back to Johnny.

Almost two metres from the first line of holes, Johnny made a second row. Soon, two lines of hazel were standing drunkenly opposite each other. Johnny touched one. It felt rough, like fine sandpaper, but pleasantly cool and alive, without actually feeling cold.

Johnny made two extra holes, in the middle between each end of rows, without Granda having to tell him. Granda nodded his approval.

Johnny paused for a little rest. His forehead was damp with sweat, but oddly, it still felt extremely hot, almost as if the mound itself was a fire, except there wasn't any fire. He was just wondering if maybe he was going down with something, and cursing his bad luck, when Granda interrupted his thoughts.

"No time for rest, laddie!" he said. He lifted a long piece of timber from the cart. There were lots of holes drilled through. Johnny held the far end and watched as Granda began bending the tops of the hazel rods into the holes of the long plank. Soon there was a semi-circular tunnel of wands supported with the plank.

"I can do it on my own now," Granda announced. "Go do something useful. Fetch some more wood, or look for dry heather or bracken for the bed. Or keep your eye on yon wee 'uns elsewise," he said, indicating Cathy and Ewen.

But Johnny was far too interested in the way Granda made the tent. He was vaguely aware that Cathy and Ewen were back and watching, too. They were all used to living in a Traveller's trailer caravan, but the old ways still fascinated.

"I know what you're going to do next," Cathy said, but stopped at one of Granda's severe looks.

Then Johnny felt the burning on his head again. He turned to look at the edge of the mound where Gran was busying herself.

"Have you made a fire, Gran?" he asked, but saw she was only just lighting one, so the heat couldn't be coming from there. Yet the heat was there right enough, as if he was leaning far too close to a flame..

Gran held out the kettle for Ewen to hang it from the saster so they would soon have a cup of tea. Then she turned to help Granda, handing him old blankets which he lay over the framework. As Granda lay them over, Johnny pulled them tight whilst Granda pinned them with home-made blackthorn pins.

Johnny never stopped being amazed at how a few sticks and scrap canvas could be made into a shelter which was warm on the coldest winter days yet cool in summer.

He passed Granda the old tobacco tin in which the blackthorn pins were kept. Granda took a handful and put them carefully into his mouth.

"Oh, you'll prick yourself!" Cathy gasped.

Johnny shook my head to reassure her. "He won't, he's done it hundred of times."

Canvas came next, thrown over and weighted down with rocks from the shore.

"We're getting there!" said Granda. "You got the bedding, Johnny?"

"I'm going now."

Johnny took Ewen's hand and Granny grabbed Cathy's. Johnny realised it was in case she fell on the rough ground, but knew she resented it from the grim look she gave Gran. Johnny reached the top of the mound with Ewen, and felt the heat more than ever, as if a hot sun was beating on his face. No, not all his face, just his forehead. But as he moved down the far side and through the rowan copse, the heat lessened.

In the rough fields alongside the narrow track, large bundles of dry bracken stood defiantly amongst the sparse grazing grass. Granny cut several armfuls with her pocket knife and Johnny and his sister and brother picked them up.

When they each had a big armful, they took them back. Granda had got the fire going and the kettle was nearly boiling.

Now Granda was standing in the sea, laying a line of mackerel hooks. Johnny stood at the edge of the water and watched Granda. Working shorewards, Granda tied a hook to the line, and from it a gaudy feather, about every forty centimetres.

Johnny tore off his shoes and socks, and lay them near the water's edge, but not near enough for the splashing waves. The pebbles were both sharp and bumpy on his feet, making him hobble until, every two or three steps, he found the relief of a flatter rock.

He picked up the end of the mackerel line, and copied, wondering if Granda would tell him to leave it to him. But he didn't need to. In a few minutes, the cold water made his fingers stiff and aching, so that tying became impossible. Yet Granda's leathery hands seemed unaffected by the cold, and kept twisting and knotting and soon there were perhaps twenty hooks and feathers dangling from it. Then they clamped the line to bits of cork so it half sank. Johnny knew that, in the heaving water, the feathers would look like small fish and the mackerel would snatch them and be caught on the hooks.

Johnny splashed back to the shore, his teeth chattering. Gran threw him a towel, and he rubbed his cold legs and ankles until they became hot. Then he went to the fireside and all but thrust his hands in to warm them.

Gran was seated beside the fire, her legs tucked under her long black dress and white apron. She started the inevitable foul pipe going, then pulled coloured tissue paper from a bag. For a few moments, Johnny watched her twist the coloured paper round short pieces of wire, to make beautiful paper flowers. Next day, he knew, she'd take them round the houses to sell.

He was about to help by wrapping green round for the stems, when Granda called from the sea, about a hundred metres further on from where he'd laid the mackerel line.

"Johnny!"

Gran told Cathy and Ewen to make the beds with the bracken, knowing they would spread the bracken out and cover it with blankets to make a soft mattress for the night.

Then Johnny pulled off his shoes and socks again to join Granda. The water was cold, but didn't feel as bad as before, as he splashed through the shallows to Granda. Still Johnny gasped.

Granda pointed down, and everywhere the seabed seemed to be coloured with the blue black of mussel shells. They felt sharp on his feet, and he wished he'd thought to keep his shoes on this time, even though they would get wet.

"Here laddie, after tea, you can pull some of them shellfish," Granda ordered. "But mark ye, make sure they're fresh. We dinnae want food poisoning."

His forehead was burning again. He reached into the water to splash it onto his head. But as he looked down, he thought he saw a face, reflected in the water. Not his face, or Granda's, but the face of a man. A man with huge eyes that seemed to glow red in the water.

"Oh!" he cried and leaped away.

"Shells cut you, laddie?" Granda asked.

"No, it was just that I thought — I thought I saw — it doesn't matter," he ended. <u>It sounded so silly. How could a face be in the sea?</u> He gazed again into the water. The face had gone.

"Nothing," he concluded.

His forehead felt hotter now than ever.

Chapter 2

Tea was fried bacon with thick bread slices wrapped round. The bacon tasted smoky from the fire. It was the best Johnny had ever had.

Afterwards, he went for the mussels with the others. The water was bitterly cold, and even though he'd already experienced it so knew what to expect, it came as a shock and he gasped. The others screamed, half in delight and half in genuine pain. But he found it hard to concentrate, because every time he looked down into the sea he expected to see that strange face again.

But he didn't, and soon his mind drifted from the face. The pebbles and patches of grit from the ground-up shells were sharp, too, and he had to concentrate hard and try to step onto rocks and not onto the shells, because his feet felt as if they were actually being cut.

There were plenty of mussels about. Ewen collected almost none, preferring to skim stones.

"Go that way," Cathy ordered Johnny. "The best ones will be there," she pointed to deeper water.

"Why?" Johnny asked.

"Because they will," she answered as if every one knew. "Honest, Johnny, you know nothing."

He wasn't sure whether or not she was right, but decided against arguing. The water was too cold and he just wanted to gather some quickly and get back onto dry land.

Cathy seemed to be right, and they soon had a bagful of large, shiny purple shellfish.

It was whilst he was bending and pulling a particularly good bunch of large ones free of the rocks where they had fastened themselves, that his forehead began to feel odd again. At first, it was only uncomfortable. Then once more, it began to burn.

He stood straight and touched his forehead. The heat was colossal. <u>Maybe I'm sickening for something</u>, he thought. <u>That'd be awful when Granda's taken us travelling in the old way</u>.

He splashed cold sea water on his head to cool it down. It helped, but not a lot.

It was then that he noticed the ram.

It was standing on the shoreline, shallow water lapping its feet, looking out to sea and no more than ten metres away, exactly where they'd first been collecting the mussels, before Cathy persuaded them to go into the deeper water

At the sight of the huge ram, he was glad they were in water which was probably too deep for it. At any rate, if it did try to get near, the wool would get heavy with water and slow it up.

For this was no ordinary ram. It was positively huge, like a great fat wolfhound. Its wool was blizzard white. But the most frightening feature was its features. It almost seemed to bear an expression of contempt. As if Johnny was someone, or somewhere, that the sheep disapproved of. And its eyes weren't the soft brown of most sheep, or the blank brown of the more stupid ones, but red. Bright red, like rock-hard rubies. Deep red. Unnaturally red. And then there was the smell. A strong reek of wet wool, drying at a fire. No, not drying — scorching, yes, that was it, Johnny realised. Like when you hang your jumper over a chair to dry and leave it too near.

The ram gazed at him. It exuded malevolence. He felt the hatred at those eyes which stared straight at him. They neither moved nor blinked. But the way they stared felt like spears piercing him.

Suddenly, he felt afraid. Not because he feared a sheep, because it wasn't that. It was something else. Something awful, like meeting a nightmare face to face. Like finding something which was out to harm you, yet which you couldn't protect yourself from. As if the face in the water had somehow turned into a monstrous animal.

The eyes seemed to be poking a way into his very mind. He imagined the sheep speaking to him.

"You have no right to be here. You know that. Why have you come?"

Johnny felt he wanted to answer, but how could you answer a thought.

We have the right, he thought. We're harming no-one. We only want to stay here to find out about the old ways. That's all.

"You have no right here. You must go. It is not your place."

"You're just a silly old ram, he thought again. We're not afraid of you. But he was.

"You have even brought back the two little ones and the old man. That is not right. This is between us. Not them. Send them out of harm's way."

Johnny thought of his younger sister and brother. He snapped himself out of the foolish thoughts and looked round to find the others and make sure they were safe. Ewen was nowhere to be seen. Cathy was back in the shallows about fifty metres further along and towards the camp, still collecting. She probably hadn't seen the ram.

"Ewen!" Johnny shouted. "Where are you?"

The ram continued its sinister stare.

"Cathy!" he called. "You seen Ewen? There's a big ram!"

She shrugged, but he wasn't sure if she was saying she hadn't seen Ewen, or 'so what? I've seen the ram and it doesn't bother me!'

When he looked back, the ram was no longer there. He glanced towards the shore. A few sheep tugged at the sparse shore grass. But the ram was nowhere to be seen.

It can't have just vanished!" he thought. "But where is it? It looked a vicious old thing. Maybe it's in a dip on the shore."

But it wasn't a satisfactory explanation. There were no dips. And were the thoughts he'd had from the ram really thoughts, or just imagination. It had never happened before, and he'd seen lots of bad things from lions in zoos to vipers at his feet, let alone vicious dogs.

"There should be enough here!" he said aloud, to break the cold silence. He splashed through the shallows, reluctant to go onto the shingle shore in case the ram reappeared.

"Let's go back!" he said as he reached Cathy. "Where's Ewen"

"There of course!"

Johnny turned and saw his little brother ambling along the shingle, occasionally picking up a stone and throwing it with gusto into the sea and making a bomb exploding sound through his lips.

"Come on!" Johnny called, and beckoned for him to hurry. Johnny kept looking round in case the huge ram reappeared.

As they picked their way through the shallows, Johnny said, "Did you see that massive ram? A nasty bit of work. I thought it was going to charge!"

"What ram?" Cathy was studying the seabed and occasionally picking out shiny looking and coloured stones. "Look what I found," she said. She held a small gold coin in her hand. Johnny hardly glanced. He doubted if it was anything very special and anyway, the sight of the ram was too fresh.

"What ram?" she repeated.

"That great big one of course! Huge thing. More like a bull than a ram. Pure white. Staring out at me. Stood on the beach!"

"I never saw one!"

Johnny sighed. "You don't use your eyes. There was one. You'll find out if it choses to charge you!"

Ewen came pell-mell along the shore to catch them up. He'd pushed his shoes back on, and his socks hung out of his pocket like little banners. His feet crunched on the beach.

"Look what I got!" he said. He held it up.

It was a handful of soggy and dazzlingly white sheep's wool.

"Where... where did you get it?" Johnny asked. He feared the answer. Ewen was so mischievous and fool-hardy it would have been just like him to have tugged it actually out of the ram's back.

"There!" Ewen pointed. "The sea kept pushing it onto the shore."

Johnny turned to look. It had come from the exact spot where the strange ram had stood and glared at him.

Chapter 3

"It's fine quality right enough! Clean, too!" Granda rubbed his thumb over the wool before handing it back to Ewen.

"But is it from a ram?" Johnny insisted. "Cos all the sheep look so grubby, but this ram looked like it'd been through a laundry."

"I never even saw a ram!" Cathy sounded scornful.

Ewen held up the wool. "I found it just on the shore line. Like it'd fallen off!" He rammed the wool in his pocket. Johnny couldn't help wondering how long it'd stay so white in the depths of a store of bits of stone, grit, sweets and all the other things Ewen tended to keep "just in case".

"I'm not so sure!" Gran hadn't seemed to be listening to the conversation. She was sitting in the opening of the bender, puffing away at her old stumpy black pipe, and sending clouds of noxious smoke to join the less obnoxious stick fire's.

It was much warmer inside the tent, and Johnny shuddered at the thought of how cold the wind had become as the evening drew on.

"What Gran?"

Johnny's brother and sister were ignoring her and chatting about this and that, lying on the blanket at the back of the bender. Johnny wanted to hear her.

"I was saying, maybe it *is* from a ram. Maybe it's from an Eelreally! You thought of that?"

Granda groaned. "Aakhh! You and your ghosts! Whoever heard of a ghost sheep? Frighten you with its baas, eh, you stupid old noodle?"

"You can scoff, you can sneer!"

The smoke from Granny's pipe grew blacker. "If that's an Eelreally, it'd explain why our Johnny seed it one moment and not the next! And no-one else seed it!"

"What, a ghost leaving it's wool behind? You'll be telling me ghosts leave bones next. Huh!" Granda rubbed his hand over the dog's head. It lay in the porch-like entrance to the bender. It was not allowed to sleep beside people but in old Traveller fashion lay as entrance guard. There was a strict order about where people slept in the tents. After the dog, the strongest man. House dwellers sometimes attacked Travellers in the night. The dog would give early warning and Granda discourage further bother with a hammer.

"If that's an eelreally, something'll happen," said Gran. "You knows the old ways as well as me. And I said eelreally, not some silly old ghost what people thinks they seed. You knows the difference as well as me."

"What?" Johnny asked.

"What what?" Gran's words plopped out with puffs of horrible smoke.

"What *is* the difference between a ghost and an eelreally."

She took the pipe from her mouth. "Eelreallys is usually good. They're ghosts what need help 'cos they're stuck here. They comes to you in dreams and oft-times something happened to them when they was alive. If you helps 'em, they're usually all right. And eelreallys is often our own flesh and blood. That's also why they comes and shows theirselves as real people and wait for their own families from these times to appear. But ghosts comes in all shapes and sizes. They got no despect for other folky. They all just scares decent folky for no good cause."

Johnny shuddered. "That ram didn't like me. And it didn't look human. Its red eyes glared, like it hated me."

"I didn't say as how all eelreallys is good. And if that ram's a bad one, there'll be good ones too. They'll come to you right enough if they needs you. That's nature, everything is a-balanced. Right and wrong, good and bad, bacon and rind." She gave the pipe several vigorous sucks and the black smoke wafted round him, making him cough.

"What might happen?" Johnny asked, wafting the smoke out of his eyes with his hand. He thought the ram alarming enough. He'd no wish for something else bad or surprising to happen.

"Who knows?" Gran shrugged. "Eelreallys sometimes tells you of something bad what's happened and going to happen again. It might be to someone no connection with us. And this is a sad place. I can feel it. That mound. I'd give a pound to a penny it was a wee croft. There were lots around once."

Johnny asked, "But why did they drive the people away? Why were the sheep more important?"

"Greed," muttered Granda. "The Great Sheep they called it! That's what it were. Two hundred years ago."

"That'll do me!" Gran knocked her old pipe onto her hand. A lump of something black smouldered on it, but seemed not to burn. She tossed it over the dog and out towards the fire. "I'm for sleep!"

"Gran? What happened to the people?"

"Some joined our people on the road. Some moved to other places. Some went to Canada. Some died of hunger and cold. And that's that!"

Johnny shuddered. To make sheep more important than peoples' lives seemed terrible. "That's awful!"

Gran lay on the large bracken bed with her head towards the children and her feet towards the door.

"That's how it was. Now you get to your own bed, cos I'm for mine."

Johnny watched fascinated as she threw a blanket over herself and began the ritual of the nightly modesty strip. Amidst a series of grunts and groans, pieces of clothing began emerging from under the blanket and were stacked alongside. A large, sack like, nightie was dragged under the covers, shortly followed by a large pair of woollen drawers and some thick socks. The over blanket resumed its crocodile lurches.

"But what about the ram? Was it an Eelreally?" Johnny tried.

"Maybe, then again maybe not! Now its time you was asleep, too. Night's not the right time to talk of such things. You peg out the mussels?"

Johnny recognized it as a ploy to divert his attention from the traveller ghost. "Yeah," he confirmed, though he knew that Granny had seen him peg the bags in the sea where they'd keep alive and fresh.

"You sleep at the very back!" Granda instructed. "Case of trouble from behind!"

Again, Johnny understood why. A younger, fit person always slept at the very rear of tents to protect small children from burkers or paedos or anyone who might come to try to snatch them away.

Now Granda pinned the front canvas sheets of the bender with the blackthorn.

"Don't expect any one'll bother us here any road!" he said, as if he had guessed Johnny's thoughts.

Sitting on the bracken bed next to Granny, he stripped off his outer clothes down to a pair of white long Johns and a white vest. Lastly, he took off his cap and laid it carefully beside him.

"Ready for anything now!" he said, lying down.

Johnny clambered carefully over Cathy and Ewen. Cathy was almost asleep, Ewen was. He said something in gobbledegook as Johnny climbed over.

Lying on the big bed, on the warm blanket and under more, he felt warm and comfortable. Alongside him he put his torch in case he needed it during the night. Outside, he heard the sea singing on the shore, an occasional shrill call of a late-up gull and a gentle breeze tickling the leaves of the rowan copse until they giggled.

He thought of the events of the day, the walk to where they were, the tent — and the ram. That made him shudder. Then he dismissed it as nonsense, and thought instead of mum and dad, and imagined them in their trailer caravan home on the council site. He missed them now it was night, but he still wouldn't want to be anywhere else.

He felt the rough blankets under and over him, and was aware that with every movement, the bracken underneath crackled and sometimes dug into his back. Not uncomfortably, but just to remind him that it was there. And there was a smell, like wet socks. Ewen's, he imagined. But, no they couldn't be. They weren't even in the tent — Gran had left them outside pegged to a rowan twig to dry. Good job mum had put a spare pair in. Wait, wet wool, why did the thought crash into the front of his mind?

The thought pushed everything pleasant to one side. Instead, he saw in his imagination, a picture of the huge ram. The smell of sea-wet wool, the animal's long nose and spiky horns, over-rode everything else. He remembered it, standing there, looking only at him. It was if he and the ram knew each other, and the ram had some unfinished business to do with him. Something sinister.

"Gran?" he called for reassurance. But she seemed to be asleep already and that comforted him somewhat. If she wasn't afraid, he needn't be either.

To try to take his mind off it, he started thinking of other things. Mum always said that if you couldn't sleep, you should imagine sheep going through a gate and count sheep. You'd *soon* be asleep, she claimed, and always chuckled as she said it.

He tried, but every time, that one, huge animal stood there, overpowering the rest of the imagined flock, solid, unmoving, it's great red eyes piercing his mind. Stood there, in the imaginary gateway and prevented the sheep he was trying to count from going through. Solid, unmoving, as if it was banning him from any other thought. The last thing he remembered before he fell asleep were the huge red eyes.

Chapter 4

...In his dream, Johnny was standing and looking out to sea. Dad was out there, on the horizon, in the family's little boat. He hoped there'd be plenty of mackerel to bring back and salt for the winter.

He picked amongst the flotsam on the beach, seeking anything useful. Some pieces of driftwood, an old branch shaped like a ram's horn, a bit of wood cask from a ship, a broken plank, a piece of rope that could be split for candle wicks, he thought. He turned back towards the croft, his hands now full.

The dark grey stone croft stood out against the two rough fields beyond. The thatch on the roof was almost black with age and here and there, a tuft of rough grass grew from it. The whole thing needed rethatching, he knew, but there was no chance of His Grace agreeing that.

He stood at the edge of the shore and looked round at the ruins of the other cottages, the insides heaps of charred black timber and dust from when His Grace's men had burned them. Once, there had been several families nearby.

Now Johnny's was the only one left. Argument and pleadings had all failed for the others.

<u>And now it's our turn</u>, he thought. <u>His Grace the Duke wants us out too. So he can graze sheep on our field. So he can make room for sheep!</u>

So far, His Grace's men had made no actual attempt to throw them out.

He looked at the friendly wooden door in the centre of the front of their home. To either side, the wooden shutters covering the window holes were only left open on fine days to let in fresh air. Johnny had seen glass many times, but only rich people could afford it, like in the big houses — His Grace's, and his manager Mr. Crawford's.

Today was too cold and windy, and Gran didn't like drafts. They'd

stay shut until the weather improved.

Their home — the croft of Aakhhamuir — was perfect. It meant, The Field of the Sea. And looking round at the family's one field, it did indeed look like a rocky field which ran right down the beach and into the sea itself.

Inside the single roomed cottage, they'd spread bracken all over the floor, and it was warm in winter and cool in summer.

Alongside, an old broad rowan tree swayed in the breeze. A few more gold-orange leaves blew off and down the beach towards the sea. He saw a single berry flick towards the ground.

A thin wisp of smoke from the single chimney disappeared into the air, and Johnny wondered if that meant Gran was boiling the potatoes which they would eat later with fish. Mam, he knew, would be out in the field, bringing in the potatoes to store for the winter.

The old milk cow lifted her head from the rough grazing field and chewed thoughtfully as he approached. He tossed the wood on the pile to chop later, and went for a word.

"You're a bonny lass!" he said. He scratched her rough brown coat, then gently stroked her ears. She shook her head violently, then held it steady for some more.

"Steady, steady, Maggy!" he soothed as she tossed her great head at him. Her rough shaggy coat looked like shredded sacking. Johnny rubbed her ears, and thought ahead to the depths of the winter, when the wind would come off the sea like a scythe, slicing through every living thing. Even with a lean-to protect her from the worst of it, Maggy would suffer. She'd get thinner and thinner, even her thick winter coat offering minimal protection. That and the shortage of food would leave her with every rib showing in the spring, and barely a cup of milk a day for the family.

He shuddered at the thought of the cold and difficulties ahead. Or was it the cold, or something else — a feeling of something about to happen? Suddenly, his cheeks felt strangely hot. They always did that when he was uneasy.

"We find it tough, too!" he reminded her, trying to reassure himself. "We'll be short of food, too! There'll be little left for the spring. Then it'll all start again!"

He sighed, gave her a last rub, and turned to look out to sea.

He jumped at the sight of someone standing at the top of the shore line, between Johnny and the cottage door. It was Mr. Crawford, His Grace's factor, who managed the Duke's estates.

Mr. Crawford's hands rested on his hips, his legs splayed so that his tight white trousers pulled against his belly. His long black coat was unbuttoned at the bottom because of his belly, too. The brass buckles on his black shoes shone, and his neat three-cornered hat looked freshly brushed.

Johnny approached respectfully. "Sir!" he acknowledged.

"Sir?" Mr. Crawford said the word like a striking snake. "Sir to you sir! And the devil take you! What're you doing still here?"

"Sir," Johnny began. He bowed his head in respect, though he felt more hatred than courtesy. "We got nowhere to go, sir."

"The devil screw your cheeky head off! D'you think that's anything to do with the case? You were told to go! You and your breed of rodents. You're still here!"

Johnny tried to keep his voice calm. He mustn't show any anger or disrespect, or they would all suffer.

"Sir, my father says..."

"God's curse on your father! Fetch him here to me NOW! Let's hear what the dog's breath has to say for himself!"

Johnny thought of his father fishing out to sea. He was trying to catch enough food to salt down for the dreadful winter.

"I can't, sir. He's out in the coble."

"Hah! Stealing His Grace's fish no doubt!"

"No sir, only the mackerel, sir."

"Devil take him! You think I don't know your scum! You think I'm a fool? You think if he gets one of his Grace's salmon on his line he'll put it back?"

Johnny wished Mr. Crawford could even half know how honest they really were, despite the hunger and the cold. "Yes sir, he never..."

"God's breath boy! You do take me for a fool! But listen to me, boy! You tell your father he should've gone when he got the chance. He wants his family's skulls cracking, that's for him." He snapped his fingers like a pistol shot, making Johnny jump. "But I'll be back. You tell the vermin that! And if he or any of you rodents is still here, your father'll know the price!"

Johnny knew already. Other families, driven out of their homes. Beaten or even killed if they resisted. Their homes burned so they couldn't come back.

"Yes sir!"

Then Mr. Crawford's voice suddenly calmed, like a gust of wind dying. "Now listen, boy. You're not a bad one, that I know. Here's a half guinea for you!"

He fished in his waistcoat pocket and pulled out the gold coin. Johnny had seen one before, but only once when dad had saved enough to buy Maggy.

"You'll give him that message, won't you!"

Mr. Crawford held the coin at arms length, like you would hand a bone to a rabid dog. Johnny stepped forward one pace. He was unsure if Mr. Crawford meant it, or would suddenly snatch the coin back at the last moment. After all, there was no reason to give away so much money just to pass on a small message.

Johnny looked into Mr. Crawford's eyes. They were reddened, and he saw that the veins in his eyeball made it look as if both eyes were scarlet tinted. But despite the redness, they looked cold and sharp, as if arrows were about to fire out from them.

He gave a second more hesitant step. He held out his hand for the coin. "Thank you, sir. Thank you very much."

The slash of Mr. Crawford's hand was like a bullet. It flashed across Johnny's head. He felt the coin, wedged in the man's fingers, gash his forehead. Then there was a tinkling sound as the coin landed somewhere on the shingle.

And Mr. Crawford was laughing. A deep, sinister laugh, like someone who had just played a wonderful trick on an old enemy...

Chapter 5

...Johnny woke up. It had been an awful dream. He was so very hot, as if he was burning. He touched his forehead. It was damp, and when he touched it, he felt pain. He tried to look at his hand to see if it was actually blood. But it was far too dark to see anything.

"In any case," he thought. "That's daft! You can't get a cut head in a dream! Stupid! I must have banged it, or Ewen's thumped me with his elbow. Yes, that'll be it!" Everything in the tent seemed normal. Both Cathy and Ewen were in obviously deep sleeps. Granda was snoring, a growling rumble like thunder. He couldn't see gran, but he could hear her lips smacking together occasionally, as if she was sucking an especially good pipe of 'baccy.

"Aakhh well!" he whispered to himself turned over, and went back to sleep.

The second time he awoke, it was a fresh if cool early morning and Cathy was getting dressed.

"Granda says you got to put shorts on, but what we want shorts on for when it's this cold I don't know," Cathy grumbled.

"Because Granda says I suppose," Johnny snapped. "I thought you'd have known that."

The memory of the dream hung heavily in his mind. Even the prospect of catching a salmon for breakfast couldn't push it to one side.

Granda was outside the tent, looking out to sea.

"Ready?" he called in, and when they nodded, added, "And don't wake that young wee scamp Ewen. Fish don't like having stones thrown into their water."

Johnny and Cathy stepped gingerly past the sleeping forms of young Ewen and Gran, the bracken crackling like electric sparks as if they were determined to wake them.

Gran opened one eye. "Good job I don't need no beauty sleep these days," she mumbled.

The wind felt cold, and Granda didn't look out of place in his three-piece blue suit, scarf, flat cap and heavy boots. Granda saw Johnny staring. "Salmon are royal fish. You got to look smart for them. Got socks?" he asked.

Johnny pulled a pair from his pocket. They were actually Ewen's from the day before which hadn't fully dried. It seemed pointless to get another pair wet. The breeze on his bare legs was cold, and the damp marsh grass on the top of the shore licked them even more coldly.

As they strolled upstream from the mouth of the small river, Johnny told the others about his weird dream.

"What d'you think it means?" he asked.

In answer, Granda grasped Johnny's arm.

"Let me see your head!" he ordered. He examined it closely. "Mm," he said, "Aye, there's a small cut there right enough. And it's been bleeding. But I 'spect you was having a dream and banged it, and the dream, sort of, explained in your mind how it'd happened. I remember once in a dream, I thought I was fighting a bear. I woke up and it was your Gran. Mind you," he mumbled, "Fighting a grizzly would've been easier."

Johnny chuckled at the picture. But he knew Granda was deliberately ducking the question.

"But what about the dream? It was so real! The house was where the mound is now. And there was a rowan still. A big, old one!"

"That's what I says. Dreams does that. Churns up what's been happening in the day, like it's clearing your mind."

"It hasn't cleared my mind. I can't get rid of the memory."

He shuddered at the thought of the evil Mr. Crawford.

"It'd take more than a dream to clear his mind," Cathy said needlessly. "The saster'd be better."

Johnny thought about saying something rude back, but Granda set such a pace as they picked their way along the bank, stepping over or round small bushes whose roots reached out into space where the river had worn the banking away.

Gradually, the bed of the river rose, the river narrowed and became deeper. Near the sea it ran broad and shallow and chattered softly. But here, it rumbled as it cascaded over tiny waterfalls and swung round rocks.

"Nearly there!" said Granda, then, "Sh! There's a flatty fishing!"

Johnny stared ahead but could see no sign of a fisherman. But sure enough, round the next bend in the river, they found him, seated on a tackle box and staring glumly into the brown waters.

"Nice morning!" Granda touched his cap respectfully. "Got much, sir?"

The man gave a mumbled reply. It was obviously no. "Been fishing here long?" Granda asked.

The man mumbled something about being part of a fishing syndicate, fishing all night, rest given up. "I hope you are more successful," Johnny heard him say. His voice was soft and quiet, but foreign sounding. Then he resumed fishing, flicking the line so that the artificial fly on the end landed on the water like a mayfly. He obviously didn't wish to continue speaking to three scruffy tinkers.

Granda touched his cap and set off again. Barely a hundred metres further on, but out of sight of the angler, Granda stopped.

"This looks a good place!" he said.

The river was flowing more slowly here, the brown water looking like gently stirring gravy.

"Right, shoes and socks off, and socks on, if you sees what I mean!" Granda ordered.

Now Granda stripped off his jacket and lay on his stomach with his head and shoulders overhanging the water. "Right!" he whispered. "Into the water you two. Socks on your hands!"

"I know, I know," said Cathy.

Johnny slid from the bank. His legs had felt cold in the breeze and damp undergrowth. But the shock of the cold river water made him gasp. It was all he could do not to shout out. His bare feet scrambled on the slippery rocks until his toes got a grip. Slowly, carefully, he waded about a metre from the bank. Cathy slipped in behind him. She couldn't help a gasp either when her feet slipped into the water.

"Quiet!" Granda whispered. "You'll frighten the beasties away."

Now Granda's hands dipped soundlessly into the water near the undercut banking. His fingers twisted and trailed in the water like weed caught in a current drifting under the banking.

Johnny understood. Granda was trying to find a salmon resting underneath the overhang. But being a nervous fish, one wrong touch and it would dart off. So Granda was making his fingers weed-like.

Gradually, Granda worked his way up the banking, feeling gently each time under the overhang.

Johnny waded carefully upstream, waiting for Granda's word. He stood near the banking.

Here, it was very undercut by the water, and the smaller roots of a Rowan had been washed clean of their soil and hung under the bank like long tendrils. Whilst he was looking at them, and wondering, he saw something move. Only slightly, and for a moment he thought it must be the flow of the water against a root. But this was much thicker and lay the wrong way.

A fish!

Frantically, he waved his arms in the air to attract Granda's attention, but he didn't see and Johnny dare not shout.

He stared downstream to where Granda lay, trying to catch his eye. Granda was gradually moving his way up stream, bit by bit groping under the banking, wafting his fingers like weed so that if they touched a fish, it would not be scared and shoot away.

Suddenly, he saw Granda stiffen. Then, still slowly and gently, as if he was de-arming a massive bomb with a fuse as delicate as a rose petal, he took his hands from the water.

"Here!" he whispered, and pointed to the banking.

Instantly, Cathy splashed her way noisily over towards him. Granda glared, trying to get her to come more quietly, but Cathy ignored the look.

Granda let out a huge groan. "I ken yer a wee explosion, Cathy, but now it's gone!" he said aloud. "Cathy, you have to be quiet. Fish don't like noise. D'you here me?"

Johnny thought Granda's anger must have been heard by every fish in Scotland.

"I was being quiet," Cathy insisted. "I was quiet as anything."

"Not quiet enough. Johnny?"

At last Granda noticed Johnny's frantic wave. He pulled himself to his feet, and stepped gently up the banking to his grandson, whispering to Cathy. "You stay there!"

"I'm not sure," Johnny whispered, "But I think I can see one under the banking. It's a long way under, though."

Slowly and gently, Granda lay down. He hooked his arms over the edge of the bank, waggled his fingers, and felt underneath. Then he nodded his head, slowly and seriously.

"Your fish, son," he whispered. "You know what to do?"

Cathy, realising something exciting was happening, began splashing up the river towards them. Granda glared downstream. "Stand absolutely still!" he growled as loudly as he dared.

Granda took his arms from the river. "Very slowly, gently!" Granda lay still, supporting his chin with his hands to prevent any sudden movement which the fish might sense.

Johnny made a slow, soundless step towards the bank. His hands dipped noiselessly under the water. The socks over them felt heavy and stopped his fingers moving in the way he'd had expected.

Centimetre by painful centimetre, he shuffled his feet forward over sharp stones and bruising pebbles, aware of the river slapping the bottoms of his shorts. Once, his foot slid on a weedy rock, and though he regained his balance immediately, he couldn't avoid a slight splash.

On the bank, Granda looked as if he was about to tear his face off with the tension. He screwed his lips round to prevent any groan or cry.

Now Johnny didn't know if the fish was still there. "It'll be long gone! Not much point being careful now!" he thought. He made little attempt to prevent noise as he gave one big stride forwards. Granda glared, stood, and strode purposefully up the riverside, mumbling to himself.

"But I'll check just in case!"

Carefully, he slipped his hands under the bank. Slowly, he felt forward with the tips of his socked fingers. There was nothing there.

Johnny was about to take his hands out and follow Granda upstream, when he decided that a look might be easier than a grope. He buckled his knees and bent his head sideways until the water lapped an ear.

He saw the fish instantly. A small salmon, perhaps four or five kilograms in weight, lying just under the surface of the water and hidden by the bank overhang. It was barely a metre from him, facing upstream, its tail and back fins wafting gently in the current.

Chapter 6

Again, centimetre by careful centimetre, he waded up behind the fish so that he was at an oblique angle to it. His left hand wafted through the water until it was opposite the fish's neck. The other hand drifted towards its tail.

As gently as if catching a butterfly, his hand slipped under the fish's belly. He pushed his index finger so that the sock was pointed and slowly, oh so gently, rubbed it along the fish's belly, barely touching it, as if his finger was a tiny weed frond drifting by in the current.

Twice, three, four times, he stroked it, until he was sure the fish thought he was nothing more dangerous than tickling weed. Then, suddenly, as a cat leaps on a mouse, his hands grabbed at the fish. One just to the left of the tail, the other round the neck. At the tail, his fingers just met. At the head, they went barely a third of the way round its great girth.

And as he pounced, the fish tried to escape. He felt its muscles twisting his hands and forcing his arm away like in an arm wrestle game. But its slipperiness was no help against the grip of Johnny's socks.

He dragged it from under the bank and at the same moment felt a bad pain under his foot. He glimpsed at the water and saw clouds of brown-red rising to the surface just downstream. For a moment, he thought the fish had bitten his foot, but knew it was impossible. Could it be its mate?

The fish twisted and writhed. He was aware of Granda half shouting and half whispering something, but the struggle was too great for him to concentrate on anything but that. Already his arms felt tired and he was aware that the great creature was struggling to gain its freedom. But he was determined to show Granda, Gran and his brother and sister that he, too, was able to live the old way.

<u>No you don't</u>, he thought, <u>You're a very fine creature but</u>...

Granda shouted. This time he was aware. "Aakhh! What a fish! A Royal fish! Lift it, Johnny, lift it."

Johnny took the weight and raised the fish from the water, and instantly feeling its power. In the water, he had only been fighting its muscles. Now, the creature knew it was defending its life. And in the air, it felt much heavier than when supported by water.

Johnny gave a massive heave and threw the fish to the banking. Immediately he was after it, his splashing bringing Granda running back down the riverside. Granda was on the fish in an instant, and taking up a large stone he crashed it onto the creature's head.

The fish gave up the fight.

"Never let any creature suffer!" Granda ordered. "We all have to eat to live, but we only kill when we must!"

"I was going to, I was..." Johnny protested.

"Still, you did well!" Granda smiled. "Your first poached Royal fish! And a beauty."

"And I got one too!" Cathy held out a small brown trout for his perusal.

"How on earth..?" Johnny began, wondering how his sister had managed to catch one.

"It was easy. I told you I knew what to do," she said.

"Aye, you've both done well," Granda smiled. "But Johnny especially so. A good fish, young Johnny. Ten pounds weight I'd say. You get the gold medal, right enough."

Johnny picked up the fish. He held it up high so he could look at its head. The jaws were open, and lined with lots of short sharp teeth. He imagined if the fish had really bitten him, it could really have done damage. Then he remembered the foot, too. In the excitement, he'd forgotten the pain from the cut.

"Now let's go back!" Granda ordered. He took a plastic bag from his inner jacket pocket and slipped the trout and the salmon into it, replacing the bag into his pocket so no-one could see.

"Can't be too careful," he grinned. "There's folk thinks folk like us should-nae have salmon. Now give me your hand!" he said.

Johnny took Granda's gnarled hand and allowed himself to be helped from the river.

As soon as his injured foot touched the ground, he felt the pain again.

"I've cut it!" he said simply as he staggered to put weight on the other foot.

Granda sat him on a rock and looked under the foot. "Aye, that's a bad cut, young Johnny. I wonder what... Aakhh, that does-nae matter the now. Let's have a closer look."

Granda reached over to a nearby rock and tugged something off.

"You're going to clean it," Cathy said, as Granda began to dab the wound with dampened rolled up moss.

"This is a deep cut, son." Granda shook his head meaningfully. "If I didn't know better I'd have sworn it was a tin lid, or a knife, did this."

Johnny was aware that Cathy was lying on the bank and peering into the water.

"It is!" she said. "A brown one."

Granda didn't seem to hear, or perhaps he was too busy. He took another chunk of moss, moulded it so the top of the moss was on the outside, damped it and layed it over the cut. "Nature's cotton wool," he said, "Just until we get home."

Gently, he pulled one of Johnny's socks over it. Only then did he go to lie beside Cathy on the banking.

"Aye, you're right, as ever,." he said in a surprised way. He leaned over the banking and felt in the water. His hand came out holding something.

"What is it?" Johnny asked.

"An old highlander's dirk!" he said. "Rusty, but the cold water'll've helped preserved it. And cleaned your wound and kept badness out, I'll be bound."

He dropped the old knife on the river bank. Johnny picked it up gingerly. The handle was long, with copper bands round the hand guard, which was in the shape of a sideways letter 'J'. That end was hardly corroded at all, but had a sort of moss-green tinge to it.

"A copper handle," Granda said. "That's why it has-nae rusted," he said.

But Johnny saw that the blade was brown and worn and looked as if it might snap at any moment. It wasn't any use.

"Throw it back," Grandad ordered. "Into the middle, where it'll harm nae man nor beast."

37

But it looked old and interesting, and Johnny felt somehow drawn to the old battered dirk. He wanted to take it back to school when the holiday was over and see if his teacher could tell him anything about it. He wrapped a hanky round the rusted blade and slipped it into his belt.

"Now let's away for breakfast!" said Granda.

Out of the river, Johnny's legs felt warm. His foot was sore, but his heart laughing as they walked without speaking, past the flatty angler who was still after his first bite.

Back at the bender, he didn't mention the dirk. Not that he was trying to keep it secret, but because there were other things to think about just then. Gran put a big plaster over the cut. She and Ewen had the kettle on, and soon they were tucking into boiled salmon steaks and hunks of brown bread.

"If only our people could live like this all the time," Granda sighed, throwing a hunk of salmon to the dog.

Which is perhaps why the dog gave no warning.

"You mean by stealing!" said a voice behind the tent.

The voice sounded oddly familiar. Johnny turned to see who was there.

It was Mr. Crawford. The man in the dream.

Chapter 7

Johnny stared at him. For a moment, he had to pinch himself to realise he was indeed awake. For there was no question — it was the same man as in the dream.

The dog dropped its piece of salmon as if it had bitten his mouth. It gave one look at Mr. Crawford, snarled once, and fled, yelping, towards the rowans where it cowered.

The man's voice was identical. But something was different. Then Johnny realised. The clothes! The tight creamish trousers which had displayed his belly were replaced with a pair of brown cord. There was no long black jacket with silver buttons, instead a dark green waxed jacket. And in place of the black three cornered hat, he had a flat cap. The black shoes with the silver buckles were replaced with dark brown riding boots. In his hand, he held a carved brown walking stick with a silver guardsman's head handle and a silver point.

"You're trespassing, too." He said it as if he was stating a known fact, adding: "The sea is there, that is a stone, you're trespassing."

For a moment, Johnny didn't understand. Then he realised- the man was being sarcastic. He meant they didn't even have the right to the smallest pebble or the tiniest drop of seawater.

"We're on the beach, sir," Granda began. "No-one owns the beach."

"The syndicate owns Aakhhamuir. And all the land here. All the sea fishing rights. All the driftwood. Everything. Which means you've been stealing, and especially the salmon."

He stepped towards the fire and peered into the pot where the remains of the salmon were being kept warm.

Carefully, deliberately, his silver tipped staff hooked the cooking pot handle. Johnny wondered what he was about to do. Suddenly, he lifted the pot, and tossed it nonchalantly onto the gravel part of the shore. The side of the pan hissed as it hit the damp. It rolled a couple of times, and the remains of the salmon squelched out and onto the ground.

"Hey!" Granda shouted. "What you doing?"

"And these are stolen, too!"

The man picked up the bag of mussels and tossed them onto the fire, which hissed back angrily.

"Stop it!" Johnny couldn't help it. Mr. Crawford — if that was still his name — looked at Johnny. His eyes were cold and dark grey. They looked dry, as if they held no emotion. But he said nothing to Johnny.

Instead, he spoke to them all, as if they were all one person. "Pack up and go. You're not allowed here. Go, or it'll be the worse for you!"

He turned, and strode up the grassy mound which covered the ruins of the croft. As Johnny watched him disappear from view, he saw something else moving through the bracken towards the man. Something very large and very white, following Mr. Crawford like a dog.

It was the enormous ram. Moments later both had disappeared from view.

"Gran, Granda!" Johnny couldn't help his alarm. "That man — it was the same one in the dream. And the ram!"

"No, you probably just thought... the dream was on your mind," Granda said.

"Not at all!" Gran disagreed. "Now will you believe in the eel really?"

"It was just a man," Granda insisted. "You'll be frightening the wee 'uns out their wits soon, all this talk o' ghosts. And I never saw nae ram, just a few sheep grazing," and he indicated two or three in the distance, cropping the short sea-salted turf.

"Nor did I, but the bairn did. Don't you doubt that."

"Yes, I did!" Johnny protested.

Granda growled. "One thing's for sure!" Spirit or no, that man was flesh and blood. And he can threaten us as much as he wants. Yon beach is nae-one's land. We're staying. Even if the theekies themselves come to arrest us in a dozen police vans. We'll go when we're good and ready. And there's nae a thing he can do about it. Now, who's going hawking flowers with grandma? And who's staying here to help me look after things?"

Johnny knew what he wanted to do. It was to go with Gran, away from this place which was turning so eerie. And when both Cathy and

Ewen wanted to remain behind, he was secretly relieved.

"Then you can come with me!" Gran agreed. "I'll be glad of the company. And you can carry the stock."

So it was. In the next village, which they'd passed through on their way yesterday, Johnny carried the large basket of paper flowers. Occasionally, his foot troubled him, but it was worth it for the pleasure of the day. Now and then, Gran took bunches out and wandered up the little paths to the cottage doors. Paths lined with whitewashed sea stones, houses all with white walls and grey slate roofs.

At every house, it was the same routine. A knock on the often maroon or blue house door, then, when someone answered, "Buy some lucky flowers from the old tinker lady," she said each time. "They'll bring your heart's desires!"

Several people bought, and by lunchtime half had gone and they were at the edge of the next, very similar, village.

<u>I wish the flowers would give me some luck</u>, Johnny thought. <u>It's all getting strange and frightening. I don't understand any of it</u>. But he said nothing, realising that Gran was preoccupied with earning a little money in the old way.

By late in the afternoon, all the flowers had been sold. On the walk back to the bender, Gran went into a local shop and bought supplies — bread, tea, evaporated milk, bacon, fruit, potatoes and other essentials, including an ounce of her special black tobacco.

"Keeps me going that stuff!" she explained, stuffing some into her little pipe. She lit it, and soon clouds of putrid black smoke drifted behind.

"<u>At least it kills the midges</u>!" Johnny thought.

In the gathering gloom of evening, the family sat around the stick fire and ate a good tea, which Granda had made with, respectively, help and hindrance from Cathy and Ewen.

"That man never come back," said Granda, helping himself to about his sixth cup of tea. "But we won't have no mackerel now. Someone — and I reckon it must've been him's — pulled the mackerel line in and chopped it to bits. If there were any fish, he must've throwed them away. Honest, a man like that! All those creatures killed for nae a thing. It's wicked evil."

Johnny understood. The man was obviously wealthy. They weren't.

Every penny they needed had to be earned through hawking, or food caught in the wild. They weren't thieves at all — they simply took what they needed as long as it didn't belong to anyone. Nothing else. And how could anyone argue that the sea itself and all the fish in it belonged to a syndicate? Hadn't God given these things for all people to use? And weren't they people?

Not, he realised, in the way Mr. Crawford saw people.

Late in the evening, they settled down for the night in the same places as the previous one. But tonight, it took Johnny a long time to fall asleep. Thoughts drifted in and out of his mind.

He was tired after all the miles he had walked, and still excited about catching the salmon, but the possibility of another bad dream worried him.

And if he did dream, would it be about Mr. Crawford? And how could someone be in a dream and then appear in real life when you'd never seen them before? And how could a cut on the head in a dream have really happened? It didn't make any sense. He was still thinking that when he must have fallen asleep...

Chapter 8

...Johnny stood near the door of the croft. Dad was out in the field with Mam, getting in the last of the potatoes. His brother and sister were playing nearby in the little paddock where Maggy grazed. He put Granny's dirk back in his belt but hidden by his shirt. He'd return it later to behind the loose stone in the fireplace, where Gran always kept it.

He thought of the stories Gran told about when her Granda had been killed with the Highland Army. The Scots had marched south into England with Bonny Prince Charlie. Later, they were defeated and the Scots Army cruelly destroyed by English Redcoat Soldiers. Since then, all weapons — even a knife — had been banned. To be seen with one usually meant death by the hangman.

Beside the door, Johnny dropped the pile of sticks he had been cutting with the dirk. He was pleased with himself. There were enough sticks to weave into a good windbreak for Maggy.

He heard the horse long before he saw it, and walked over to meet the rider.

Mr. Crawford reined in the animal and jumped off. There were several other people with him, ruffians whom Johnny half recognized as from other parts of the Duke's estates. Two carried flaming torches. He knew one of these. A huge man, with something wrong with his eyes which made them look unnaturally red. Johnny had heard of the man. He was nicknamed An Reith — The Ram — by everyone. A man with a reputation as much for his cruelty as his great strength.

Mr. Crawford was wearing the same tight cream trousers as before, and his black buckled shoes shone like the sun. As he strode towards Johnny, Mr. Crawford stood in some mud which marked the side of one of the expensive shoes.

"God's curse on you scum and your mud!" he shouted. "Where's your father?"

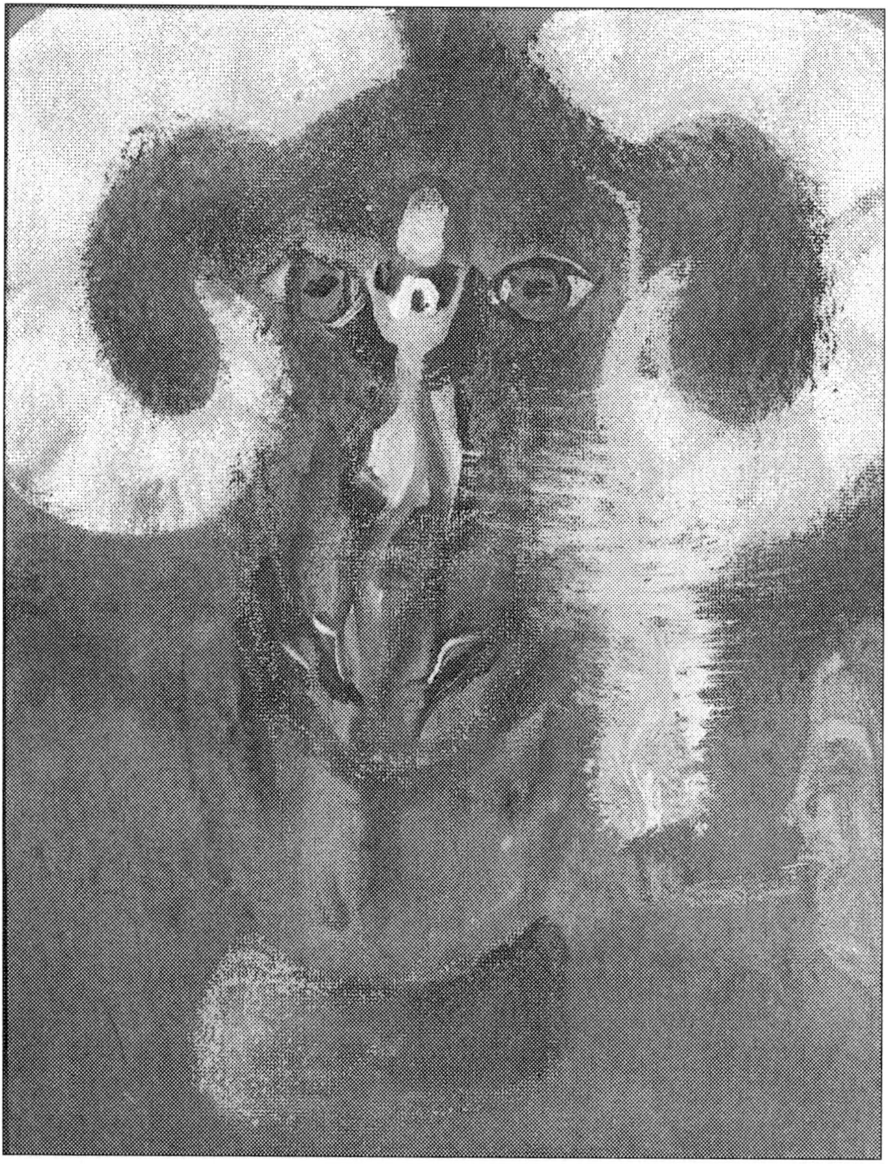

"In the field, sir, getting the tatties."

"Stealing them more like! Everything on this land belongs to His Grace, including the people. Though what he's ever done to injure God and deserve such devil's breaths as you draggletailed tinkers I don't know. Fetch your father here!"

Johnny knew he didn't need to. His brother and sister had already fled the confrontation to fetch him and ma.

"Who's in the house?" The man shouted, though he was right next to Johnny.

"Just my old Gran, sir," Johnny said. He had just seen her on her stool in her favourite place in the doorway, smoking her old clay pipe. Her black bonnet and thick plaid shawl protected her from the sea breeze.

"Tell the wizened old witch to come out and make speed about it!"

Dad arrived. Mr. Crawford turned on him.

"You're still here, MacPhee! God's curse on you! You had the order. The justices have told you to go. Now go immediately!"

"We've nowhere else to go, sir, and the winter's coming."

"Devil curse you! D'you think that's a matter for His Grace? Isn't the land his own to do with as he wishes? Get you gone, before these gentlemen carry out the court's orders."

Johnny looked at the men. Now he saw several were carrying clubs and swords.

"If we leave, we'll starve!" said dad.

"Starve? STARVE?" Mr. Crawford shouted. "You think that's any concern of ours? His Grace is turning all his land over to sheep. There's no room for scum! His Grace has to live, too, and the rent you pay a year wouldn't keep one of His Grace's sheep dogs in meat for a week! You're the last tenants in this area. You will go today. The papers are signed by the Magistrate. And may the devil take you speedily!"

"No sir, that we can't." Dad's voice was calm, but Johnny recognized the determination.

"Now listen man!" Mr. Crawford suddenly sounded reasonable. Johnny remembered what had happened with the half guinea the day before when he sounded reasonable. He had a bad feeling that something would happen. He touched the cut on his forehead.

"If you go now, his lordship will give you a handcart to move your belongings. If you go fifty miles down the coast His Grace's factor there has orders to find you a wee cottage. What d'you say?" Mr. Crawford held out his hand as if seeking to come to an agreement.

"We won't move, sir, not for you nor the minister of religion nor the duke himself. We have been faithful and loyal tenants on this land for generations, and never a reason for His Grace to be other than satisfied. We've never touched His Grace's salmon, nor his deer and partridge. No-one could have been more honourable."

"Damn your eyes and blast you to the devil!" Mr. Crawford shouted. "Haven't you understood? Your days of being here are over, man. And if you won't go when you're told, you must expect the consequences!"

"Sir, I beg you! The winter! It'll be the death of the old woman and the bairns as surely as snow falls."

Mr. Crawford shrugged. His face showed he cared nothing for their fate. He made a signal to An Reith who walked his horse slowly forward. Before Johnny could give any warning, An Reith raised a thick club and smashed it down onto dad's skull.

"No! No!" Johnny screamed. There was a splash of dark red on dad's head. His legs crumpled as if they were made of seaweed on an outward tide. Dad slumped to the floor.

"Da! Da!" Johnny cried. "You've killed my da!"

Johnny threw himself onto his father's body. The grief swelled inside him and exploded in a torrent of cries and tears. But even as the tears cascaded, he saw his father move and realised he wasn't, after all, dead. His tears changed from grief to relief.

"Get out'f the way, boy!"

Mr. Crawford pushed Johnny aside. He nodded purposefully at the man known as An Reith, The Ram. An Reith and the other man with the torch dug their heels into their horses sides. Casually, as if it was almost too much trouble, the horses strolled forward. Slowly and deliberately they approached the croft. An Reith's red eyes seemed to burn with fire.

Johnny could see what was about to happen, but his feet felt rooted to the spot. He longed to leap forward, grab the torches and hurl them into the sea.

He watched the tops of the tussocky grass, which struggled to survive just above the high tide line, bow towards the cottage. As if they were saying farewell.

Still his feet would not move.

Crawford's men threw their torches into each end of the thatched roof. The dry straw thatch caught immediately, slowly at first, smouldering, then glaring with red anger.

"Gran! Gran's in there!" Johnny called. Now the fear was back, as great as ever.

"Then she'd better get out!" Mr. Crawford's voice was calm and cold, colder than a winter sea.

"Gran! Gran!"

And suddenly, Johnny's feet ceased to be fastened down.

He set off running towards the croft door. He could hear mum and the rest of the family screaming somewhere behind him.

The flames were skipping over almost the whole roof now, like small red pixies, dancing with joy at the destruction.

Johnny reached the door. No-one tried to stop him.

"Gran! Gran!" he called.

Wisps of smoke stretched out of the doorway like fingers poaching salmon. Gran was no longer sitting there! He entered to find her. Inside was darker than usual, and he realised it was because of the thick smoke coming down through the roof and sitting underneath like a heavy grey blanket, shaking and unshaking itself with a series of thuds.

"Gran!"

At first he couldn't see her at all, and the wisps of smoke caught at his eyes and made them water, making seeing the harder.

He staggered across the croft, banging into the rough table and Gran's old rocker by the fire. The grate fire looked small and pathetic, as if it knew it was about to be out-shone by its massive sister. The burning roof roared louder than ever.

Johnny almost stumbled against Gran. She was standing in the gloom of the single room, leaning against the wall under part of the roof not yet billowing smoke.

"Gran! Come on!"

He could say no more because of his coughing. He doubled up, coughed away the smoke, and stood upright again. He grasped her arm and tried to pull her towards the grey doorway.

But she pushed his arm away. He was surprised by her strength, as if she had found new muscles on her old frame.

"No!" she croaked through the swirling smoke. "You be gone! Save yourself, laddie!"

"You must come!" he managed. "The roof! It'll fall in any time!"

Already the first flames had licked through the thatch and in the far corner, wisps of burning straw flitted down like red rowan leaves.

"This is my home! I must stay!" Gran croaked, and pushed him harder than before, so that he staggered a few steps in the direction of the doorway.

"Gran!" he called.

There was a huge crash as a pile of burning straw fell in the far corner on top of the heather beds. They caught fire immediately.

"Gran!"

The smoke swirled round him, caught in his throat and made him cough and cough.

He longed for good air, and bent down beneath the smoke canopy.

"Gran!" he coughed again.

Then, somewhere at the far side of the smoke, he heard her voice. It was no longer croaking, but soft, yet loud enough to be heard above the roaring, and smooth as new-churned butter.

"Go, Johnny my boy! I must stay. You will come back for me one day. Then I will go too. But not now. Go! Save yourself and your family. Go now, Johnny, quickly, and God be with you. And Johnny — come back one day for me! And when you do, bury me in the kirkyard. You promise! I hold you to it, my laddie!"

There was an authority about the voice. Perhaps it was the calmness, or the certainty that she would not come. He was unsure. He had no choice but to nod in agreement and stagger towards the doorway. He fled out into the air, sucking in the fresh air and coughing the smoke out in between...

Chapter 9

...It was still dark when Johnny awoke. He could hear the rain pattering on the bender roof.

But it was not comforting. The horror of the burning croft sat at the front of his mind and refused to go away. He thought of himself in the dream, and his Dream Gran, caught in her burning home. He only remembered staggering out of the house and gasping for air. It was as if he had staggered from the dream, too. But what had happened after? He half wanted to know, and half feared the answer.

"But I have to find out!" he whispered to himself. "That's what the eelreallys want me to do, I'm sure of it."

He wiped a hand over his forehead. It burned, just like when he had first seen the ram.

<u>I'll have to cool off</u>, he thought. <u>There's only one thing to do. Get a breath of fresh air and go back to sleep. Maybe I won't dream again. But in a way I hope I do.</u>

Near him, Cathy and Ewen were in heavy sleep. Gran and Granda seemed to be, too.

His head hurt. He touched it, and found it still glowingly hot, like a fire.

Like he had just been too near a real fire and not just one in a dream.

He longed to cool it. The rain! He imagined it dripping onto his hot forehead, soothing it.

Carefully, by the light of his torch, he stepped over his brother and sister, and chose a route between Gran and Granda.

Riley the dog opened one eye and gazed up at Johnny, who imagined the animal puzzling. Why should anybody want to leave the tent on a night like this when the rain lashed and the wind gusted?

"Stay, lad," he whispered and stepped over the prostate animal. Riley looked relieved, sighed, and rested his chin back onto his paws.

Outside, a gust of wind took Johnny's breath away, and the cold rain whipped his forehead.

"That's me in again," he thought to himself. "It's too cold here, and too dark." So dark that he could he see no light other than that from his little torch.

When he turned to re-enter the little tent, the torch flashed through the blackness, and as it did so caught an odd shape. If he hadn't known better, he'd have sworn it was the shape of a human, a small one. A person standing to one side of the tent and at the edge of the mound.

Even so, he flashed the torch round again, trying to convince himself that nothing could be there.

But something was there. A shape about his own height.

A shudder went down Johnny's spine. No living person could be outside on a night like this.

He flashed the torch again, convinced he would see nothing more sinister than a broken-off rowan, or a fence post.

And remembered that there was nothing there. Nothing but the edge of the mound that had once been a cottage.

He shone the torch directly onto the figure, and as the light flashed across the intruder's eyes, it raised an arm to protect them.

The shiver returned to Johnny's spine. Involuntarily, he stepped back away from the shelter of the tent. Further from the lee of the tent, the rain lashed him, the wind pushing in from the sea, trying to heave him towards the strange figure.

Johnny screamed to try to dismiss the fear and shudders and the cold from his body. The wind caught the sound and hurled it away over the mound and up into the hills beyond.

"Who are you? What do you want?" Johnny shouted. The words jerked out as the wind snatched them to throw them away again. And half answering his own question, he said, "You're an eelreally, aren't you?".

The figure spoke something to Johnny. The words were calm and soft and defied the wind, surfing through it so he could hear them plainly. But he could not actually understand what the figure said.

"Who *are* you?" Johnny challenged again. When the figure did not respond, he repeated. "Who *are* you?"

The figure said something else.

Johnny felt the shudder go down his back. If this a real person, he shouldn't be there. But if it was an eel really, a ghost ...and it had to be...

Then he remembered Riley. The family had always said that dogs could recognize a ghost. If it was one, Riley would run away in terror. That's what dogs always did. Johnny clicked his tongue against the side of his teeth. Riley stood, stretched nonchalantly, and peered out into the rain. He looked up at Johnny as if he was asking if he was *sure* he wanted him to venture out on such a night.

"Here!" Johnny said, sharply. He pointed towards the figure. "Get him!"

The dog looked vaguely towards the figure. But did not move. "Go on!" Johnny urged. If the person was real, the dog would see them off. At least he'd know for sure.

The dog's back legs and tail remained in the shelter of the bender. "GO ON!" Johnny urged. He looked again at the figure, who still stood exactly where he had.

The figure said something else. Something short, like a one-word question, as if he was calling a name.

Suddenly, Riley's ears pricked up. He gave a loud yelp, the sort a dog gives when it meets a long lost friend. He leaped out of the tent and ran, full of obvious joy, towards the figure. But at the last moment, he crouched down and whimpered, as if he wasn't sure if he was correct or not.

The figure spoke again.

"Riley!" Johnny called to the dog, to fetch him back from this unknown and strange reaction. "Come here!"

Johnny shuddered again. This time, not so much through fear as cold. For it was colder now than he ever remembered it. But after all, he reasoned, if Riley wasn't scared, he needn't be either, and the cold was just because of the wind and rain.

But the dog ignored him. It was crouched down now, near the mysterious figure, whining and fawning. It was almost as if it sought forgiveness from the mysterious person.

Johnny gave another involuntary shudder of cold. He could not understand why the dog acted in this way.

"Riley! Come!" He almost shouted the command, but although he clearly saw one of Riley's ears bend back in acknowledgement in the torchlight, the dog continued its fawning as if to a long lost friend.

"Riley!"

Johnny was almost shouting now.

Then Johnny thought, <u>Maybe this is a dream too. Maybe I'll wake up in a moment.</u> He stretched out to touch the side of the bender, realising that if he felt something, it had to be real.

It was horribly non-dreaming. The rough blanket felt wet and cold. In any case, hadn't the wind and the lashing rain on his burning forehead proved he was very much awake?

"Who are you?"

The figure began to speak. It was a mix of the old Scots language interspersed with English and the travelling peoples' own Cant. That much he could tell. But the accent and some of the words themselves made it incredibly difficult to understand what he was saying. All he could understand were, here and there, odd words and occasional phrases. And every few seconds the same two words, said over and over:

"Aakhhamuir... help. Fire... Crafford... fire... fell... Crafford... horse... fell... fell down... ran... Crafford... fire... help... Crafford... help... Gran... help... Aakhhamuir... the kirkyard."

Chapter 10

The wind lashed at the words, hurling them away from the ruined cottage.

But Johnny could understand and hear enough to realise what the figure was saying. He was a ghost all right, an eelreally. And he had been waiting for someone to come here. Anyone? Or a particular person?

He wanted help. Help to find his Gran who lay somewhere in the ruins. And help to do something for him, though Johnny could not then understand what.

And all the time, Riley the dog lay at the eelreally's feet, showing no sign of fear. Instead he displayed joy at being next to the figure.

It was this which allayed Johnny's own fears. For if the dog was not scared, he needn't be either.

The figure stood and stared at Johnny, as if it wanted a reply. Johnny wasn't sure what to say. He'd help if he could, but he wasn't sure how.

"What do you want me to do?"

He heard enough of the reply to understand: He would know when the time came.

The figure spoke again for a long time and once more Johnny found he words difficult to follow:

"Dream... seek... Aakhhamuir... rocks and stones... turf... bones... kirk yard... seek..." And last, he heard plainly, "seek also for me."

The figure stopped suddenly. If it had been human, Johnny swore later, the blood draining from the face made it whiter. But eelreallys had no blood. Still, the figure's face looked white, frightened. It held up an arm and pointed. Pointed towards Johnny but beyond him. The eelreally's voice was even harder to understand now, for it was suddenly filled with what Johnny realised were strange words gabbled in terror.

But two of the words, said over and over, were clear enough. "An Reith, An Reith!"

Something was scaring the ghost! Something behind Johnny which the ghost had seen.

Johnny felt utter fear trickle down his back. He swung round, unsure what horror was behind. And saw it immediately. There, trotting through the wind and rain apparently straight at him and the bender tent, was the huge white ram. Its head held high, with red eyes latched on Johnny and glaring through the gloom. White froth bubbled from the sides of its mouth.

Johnny screamed again, but had no time to leap aside. Instead he gazed, fear freezing him to the spot, as the ram trotted silently on. It began to run and lowered its massive horns to butt and batter and gore anything in its path.

Johnny, still frozen in fear, waited for the inevitable crash as the huge creature neared and then the miracle. At the last moment, almost as Johnny expected to feel the spray of its white frothed breath, the animal seemed to swerve, past Johnny and the tent.

Johnny gazed after it, still rooted where he stood. Riley gave a yelp of fear and scooted to one side. Then the huge ram was at the eelreally boy and about to crash into him. And then, like a movie still, the two figures froze into statues. Statues of a boy and a ram which became vague and gradually faded away until nothing was left but the memory. And the last to go were the ram's red eyes, and the boy's hand, waving, as if in sad farewell.

Riley the dog turned, suddenly, as if he had been told to go back.

"Wait!" Johnny shouted after the eelreallys. "Come back! The ram! What does it all mean? Are you all right? Your name! What is it?" he added as an afterthought. For he was sure he knew, and if the suspicion was right then the figure could only be the Johnny of the dreams who had lived here all those years before.

And the ram was somehow to do with the time of the Great Sheep, when wool was considered more important than people.

"Wait!" he called again.

Then there was nothing at all there. Only the mound and the wet tent side, and the ever present gusting wind and lashing rain.

And through the wind came the howling of Riley the dog, a wretched wailing that its long lost friend had gone again.

Johnny stood in silence for a few minutes. Then he was suddenly aware that he was cold, and very wet. His night clothes stuck to him. His face, even the once burning forehead, ached with cold.

"Riley, come on," he called.

The dog came, almost reluctantly, and in the entrance to the tent gave a mighty shake, spraying water over the sleeping forms of Granda and Gran. Gran stirred in her sleep, and said something which could have been a swear word.

Johnny groped in the entrance to the tent and found an old towel. He rubbed it hard over Riley's back and sides and head, and the dog wagged its tail slowly. Johnny imagined it saying, <u>Thanks, but I'm not really that bothered. I'd rather be out in the rain with my old friend</u>.

"Who is that?" he whispered to the dog. "And how can you possibly know him? And what's that awful ram to do with it all."

But the dog only look into Johnny's face and wagged its tail lethargically. Then it slumped down in the front of the tent and rested its nose back on its front paws, peering out into the black night as if it hoped the visitor would yet return.

Johnny himself sighed. He picked his way back over the sleeping family and stripped off the wet clothes. He found his daytime shirt and trousers and put them on for warmth. Then he snuggled down under the blanket.

He half wanted to fall asleep, and half not to. And he also wanted to find the next awful chapter in the life of Dream Johnny, yet feared it too. He tried to convince himself that now, he wouldn't dream. He tried to turn his mind away from the events of the night.

He must have fallen asleep. But suddenly, he heard his voice being whispered and realised it was Gran. He awoke with a start, saw she wasn't right next to him, and instantly realised that something in the tent was different.

He glanced round. Ewen and Cathy were fast asleep, and he could see the muffled form of Granda and beside her, Gran. Perhaps she'd been saying his name in her sleep, he surmised. Then he realised something was different. It was the smell. Tobacco smoke, certainly, but even stronger than Gran's usual. Heavy, like a thick pungent fog which pervaded the entire tent. It had such a strong smell, it even made his head spin.

He was just going to ask Gran why she was doing something so dangerous, lying there and smoking in the middle of the night, when it could set the tent on fire. But as he was about to ask, he saw that she wasn't actually lying beside Granda. She was up, and seated on a stool in the entrance to the tent. Her foul black pipe exuded clouds of awful smoke.

She had a large plaid shawl over her shoulders, to keep off the cold, and a large black bonnet on her head. He didn't remember her wearing either thing before. And the tobacco smelt much worse than usual, as if it was thick and tarry. Outside, he could see the glow of the stick fire, just aglow despite the rain.

"Gran!" he said. "I've seen a ghost. It was a boy standing out in the rain on the mound of the cottage. And I have to help him. And before that, I had this dream. It was awful. You were in a fire, they burned the croft to get us out. Only it wasn't you and it wasn't me. It was..."

His voice petered out. It was Gran sitting there, it could only be, yet it wasn't quite. For a start, they didn't have a stool in the tent, yet she was on one. And the figure, though looking very like Gran, certainly, — the same eyes and nose — was older looking and more worn. And the hair, although grey like real Gran's, showed streaks of red.

Chapter 11

He shone the torch back where Gran was lying. There was a bulge, but he knew she couldn't be there! This was Gran for certain. It could be no other. There couldn't be two Gran's, or a gran and a..."

He refused to allow himself to even think of the word ghost. One human and one animal ghost in the course of the night was enough. Ghosts were something that should stay in books and haunted houses. Or even outside like Dream Johnny. But never in Granda's tent. Not looking so like Gran herself.

Johnny gazed at the Dream Gran's face.

"Am I awake?" he whispered to himself. He tapped the torch on his hand, and felt it. "Am I?" He dug his nail into his arm. It hurt.

The Dream Gran smiled. "I knew you'd come back for me!" she said. "But it's been a long time, oh so long."

Her voice sounded tired, as if it needed to rest. Her accent was thick Scottish and he found her hard to understand. Her accent was exactly like that of the figure outside. Not like in the dream, where he understood every word.

"Who are you?" he whispered. "Are you an eelreally?"

She smiled again. "The truth is I dinna know. But if I am, I'm nae a wicked one, that you can be assured of."

Johnny couldn't help a shudder. "You might be an evil ghost. You might be going to harm us!"

He was beginning to find her smile disarming, as if she felt she was talking to an imbecile.

"Your dog. See, it lies there near me, with nae a bit of fear. It knaws its ane family. For dogs —" She said the word dogs as if it was dags — "knaw evil and good. And see, it has nae fear, nae fear at aw! If I was evil, would it nae hae set up a barking to wake the very dead?"

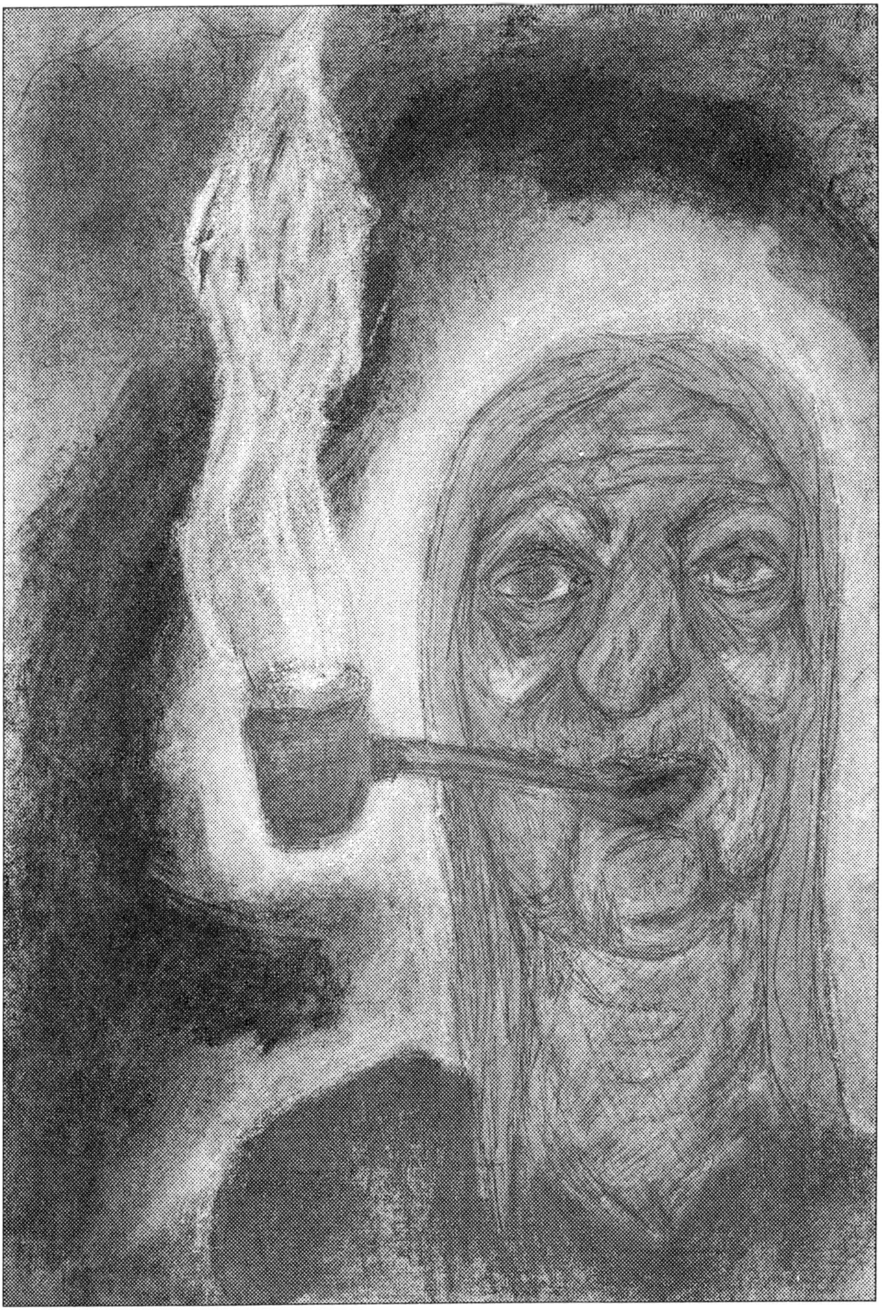

Johnny knew this was true. If dogs detected an evil spirit, they ran off yelping for no apparent reason. All dogs did it, and all Travelling people knew it for a fact. And Riley hadn't been scared of the boy ghost — it had welcomed him like a long lost friend. And it wasn't afraid of the old woman.

"The boy. Outside. Is that your grandson?"

The old woman looked puzzled for a moment. Then, "I see you ken the truth," she said. "Though I would hae hoped you would recognize me onyway. Oh Johnny, my Johnny! Ye havenae changed over all these years. Surely I havenae either. Or is it that ye are — o' course yer ane family."

She sighed. "But then, that was sae long ago. Perhaps even though we are aw gone, and seem timeless, we change! Who knows? But now my Johnny, ye must heed ma words. Ye are in terrible danger. Last time, when ye tried to help the family here, at Aakhhamuir, ye failed. This time you mustn't."

He was confused. "Last time? But there's never been a last time! Unless it was ......" He thought he understood what she meant. She was confusing him with Dream Johnny. One minute realising he wasn't, then forgetting. That's why she'd looked puzzled when he mentioned her grandson.

"Aakhh!" she sighed. "Memory is only a cart wheel which rolls through time. Yours has broked on the rock o' grief. Maybe it was yer young years. Or maybe, aye maybe, ye are the relative come to help us. God pray ye are."

She sighed and puffed again on the foul pipe. "Ye must try to remember, for ye are in terrible danger. Crafford, he will come again. This time, do not repeat your mistake. And when it's over, seek for me in the rubble and bury me decently, my Johnny. And seek your ane past and do as ye must."

Another shudder went down Johnny's back. Seek for her? For his own past? But if she was from the past, she must mean bones, a skeleton, there somewhere near the tent. In the mound. Which was exactly as the figure had said to him outside. Only the figure had wanted him to seek for something else, too.

"Please listen," Johnny pleaded. "I don't really understand what's going on. But I am not your grandson. Maybe I am a relative, but it is

200 years since the days of the Great Sheep and Mr. Crawford and An Reith."

"Aye, aye," the old woman nodded. "I keep forgetting right enough. Two hundred years is a long long time to remember every detail. If ye are nae my Johnny, then by heaven itself ye are very like him. And so ye must have come here to help us. Which is all we want."

"Yes, I thought that. But I still don't understand it all," he said. "What..."

"Shush, my Johnny. Ye will understand. Only be patient." Her voice was very soft and gentle now. Like a lullaby on the breeze, in the rain. "Oh, how I've waited for this time. Ye remember the old lullaby? That I used to sing to ye and the other bairns sae long back?" She began to sing, softly, like a breeze through a summer sycamore.

"Sloom, sloom, mo chawvi,
"Klisn loork, klisn loork,
"Stawl asloom array been kam
"Array kam array mo fambel."

He had never heard such words before, yet he understood, as surely as if they had been spoken by Cathy or Ewen or anyone.

"Go to sleep, go to sleep my boy, close your eyes, close your eyes, sleep deeply and in peace, in the love that I have."

His mind was bubbling with questions. "But..." he began...

...He didn't remember going back to the bed. Or going to sleep. Or dreaming anything else...

...He awoke on a dry, sunny but cool morning, with seagulls wheeling and screaming overhead in sheer joy at being alive. There was a smell of frying bacon, and when he pulled on his clothes and came from the tent, the others were seated round the fire, tucking into great slabs of bacon sandwiches.

"Aakhhhh! Here's the late waker at last. Go have a wash in the stream, then come for breakfast," said Gran.

Johnny looked at her. He thought of the Dream Gran and stared at real Gran's face. It was very like Dream Gran's. The eyes, the nose. Only the hair. Real Gran's was grey, but still with black streaks. Dream Gran's grey with a hint of red.

"Go on!" she repeated.

"I had another funny dream!" he said. "It was the croft, and Gran..."

"Go and wash the sleep from your eyes and dreams from your memory," said Real Gran, "Then come and eat. The day's too nice to talk of things of the night."

He wanted to tell them about the second odd dream, but somehow it didn't seem the right thing to do. And to explain about seeing a ghost Gran in the tent would probably have scared Cathy and Ewen rigid. Real Gran was right. This wasn't the right time. He sighed, decided to wait until later, and went for the wash.

He was shaking the cold spring water from his hands when he heard the Landrover. A deep dread, a blackness of despair and fear, swept over him. And he knew deep within him that the moment had come. The time that Dream Gran had mentioned when he must this time do the right thing. Whatever that might be. And that, somehow, Mr. Crawford and the red eyed ram were involved, and putting them all into an unknown but fearsome danger.

Chapter 12

Mr. Crawford parked his Landrover on the top of the beach. He was holding a bottle in his hand.

The man walked to the fire. Gran and Granda stood to meet him. Cathy and Ewen fell silent.

"So you're still here. Well, I'm tired of waiting. You're trespassing, you dirty tinkers. You have no right here at Aakhhamuir. And you're going. Now. Whilst I watch. Or it'll be the worse for you!"

Johnny couldn't stop himself. "We're not dirty tinkers." He held up his newly washed hands in evidence. "We're clean, and we're travelling people. We're harming no-one!"

"Keep the brat under control!" Mr. Crawford snapped at Granda.

"The boy's right. We're no dirtier than you. And we're not moving! We're on a public beach and harming no a soul!"

Mr. Crawford sighed. He walked casually over to the bender. At first Johnny didn't know what he intended. And then he realised! The dream! The bottle! He was going to burn them out. In the dream, Johnny had failed to stop the tragedy with the croft. When Dream Gran had died.

What was it Dream Gran said? Yes, 'This time when Crawford comes, do not repeat your mistake.' This time he wouldn't.

Mr. Crawford was nearly at the tent. He raised the bottle, and Johnny knew that he would smash it on the wooden rafter of the tent. Then petrol, or paraffin or whatever would spill out. He would drop a match, and...

But not this time. Johnny ran at Mr. Crawford like a charging ram. He butted his side with his head. Mr. Crawford lost his balance, and the bottle of petrol — Johnny could smell it now — smashed on the ground, not the tent. But it splashed up, onto the tent, Mr. Crawford and onto Johnny.

"You stupid oaf!"

Mr. Crawford regained his feet and lashed out at Johnny.

Johnny heard Gran shout, "Leave him alone!"

He backed away from Mr. Crawford, making a wide berth round the fire. But as Mr. Crawford reached the fire, he snatched a burning stick and, glancing back, threw it, deliberately, onto the petrol at the side of the bender.

It caught immediately and flames rushed up the tent.

"This time, do not repeat your mistake!" The words were there, suddenly, as if Dream Gran had actually shouted them.

But it was too late. He had already failed!

The anger, the despair, the black hopelessness of it all rose in him.

"You wicked wicked man!" he shouted.

He leaped on Mr. Crawford with such force that the man fell over. They rolled over on the ground. Then Mr. Crawford, being the stronger, was on top of him. He slapped Johnny across the face — once, twice, three times.

Something was hurting Johnny's side, where the man's weight pressed on him. His hand tried to move whatever caused the pain and closed over the old dirk. He pulled it from his belt, where it had remained since he found it. He did not intend to use it, but simply to remove the pain from his side.

"This time, do not repeat your mistake!" The words swirled through his mind like a wind.

He raised his daggered hand as high above Mr. Crawford as possible to strike. He had no wish to, he couldn't understand his own action. But the hand holding the knife no longer seemed to be his. It was as if it was someone else struggling with Mr. Crawford, someone he only half knew. Mr. Crawford was chuckling, as if he was enjoying hurting the boy.

"THIS TIME, DO NOT REPEAT YOUR MISTAKE!" The words screamed in his head, hammering on his skull as if they were trying to escape.

"THIS TIME, DO NOT REPEAT YOUR MISTAKE!"

Then the knife was snatched from his hand. And Real Gran was there, shouting at him.

"No! No!"

He could hear Cathy and Ewen crying somewhere in the background.

And suddenly, Mr. Crawford fell off him and rolled to one side. It was Gran to the rescue again. She threw the saster iron to one side. Mr. Crawford was rubbing his shoulder. Then Gran picked up a bucket of water and threw it over Mr. Crawford.

"Get up!" she ordered Johnny. "Knives aren't for hurting people. No matter what!" she snarled. She bent her arm back and threw the knife so hard that the blade whistled a low note as it spun over the fire, over the rowans and to the small river beyond. Johnny imagined it splashing into the water.

And then there was another voice, a strange one, with a foreign accent.

"Mr. Crawford, what is going on?"

Johnny regained his feet. The speaker was a man in a brown tweed suit. The man who had been fishing at the river when they got the salmon and trout and the man could catch nothing.

"They're dirty tinks, sir, I'm trying to get them shifted. They attacked me!"

"It looks rather to me as if it was you attacked a boy much smaller than himself. And how did their tent catch fire?"

"I don't know Herr Breitmann! It's nothing to do with me!"

"Yes it was, liar!" Johnny shouted. "He put petrol on."

The smart man held up his hand for silence. "I think, Mr. Crawford, you should go now and get changed. Your clothes are filthy from rolling on the shore. I shall see you later. I wish to speak to these people."

"We're doing no harm sir! Just stopping here a few days. Showing the youngsters the old travelling ways of our people," said Granda, as Mr. Crawford skulked away. Johnny was vaguely aware — or was it only imagination — that a huge ram was following the man. But this time, an animal which could barely be seen, as the sunshine seemed to shine through it like a window.

"I know you're harmless," said Herr Breitmann. "But I'm afraid your tent's had it. First, tell me everything that's happened." He sat on the upturned bucket Gran had just used to wet Mr. Crawford.

And they explained the events of the past few days, but Johnny especially described the dreams.

"I see," said the man, "Or I think I do. You've had a bad time here. And it sounds as if some terrible evil was done here in the past. But Mr. Crawford is right in one thing. Aakhhamuir is mine. Even the beach is. And I have the rights to the salmon and the trout in the burn. However, you are welcome to stay here. And I don't mind you taking the odd fish, either. There's plenty for everyone. At least you can catch them, which is more than me!"

"As to that, sir, I'd be honoured to fish alongside you. Only we can't stay now, sir," sighed Granda. "We've lost the tent and everything in it."

"This might help!" Cathy handed something to Granda. Johnny saw it was the gold coin she'd found.

"Let me see!" said Mr. Breitmann. "Ah, a gold half guinea. 1780. English. And in remarkably fine condition. Where did you find it?"

Johnny said, "Mr. Crawford in the dream threw it," at the same time as Cathy said, "On the beach, over there! Johnny touched the scabbed mark on his forehead.

Mr. Breitmann handed it back to Cathy. "Whether it's worth much I don't know. But I can help anyway. I own all the land round here, not just Aakhhamuir. It's a syndicate uses it. Shooting, fishing, that sort of thing. You're welcome to stay as long as you want. I'll make sure none of my people bother you."

"But we've no tent!" Johnny reminded him.

"I realise. I'll send down some more canvas and new blankets later today, too. And some food. And I think we can find some old clothes to help you out for those you've lost in the fire. I've got children of my own."

He smiled broadly across at Ewen and Cathy, and warmed his hands over the fire.

"Thank you, sir, thank you very much!" said Granda. Through the smoke, he shook the gentleman's hand.

"And from what this young man says," he said, indicating Johnny, "I think we should search the mound. I have a feeling we'll find bones there that ought to have a proper burial."

Chapter 13

The canvas smelt new. So did the blankets. And the hazel smelt fresh-cut.

Johnny had watched for much of the afternoon as a procession of people sent by Herr Breitmann brought the things they needed to set up a new bender. One or two bits were savable from the remains of the old tent, but most were charred and useless.

Lying upon the newly made bracken and blanket bed, Johnny stared up at the new blanket-lined roof above him. Sleep was nowhere near. After all, so much had happened during the day. It had been a good day, all in all, despite his mistake in fighting Mr. Crawford. But at least he hadn't done anything so foolish as to stab him.

In the doorway of the tent, both Gran and Granda were sitting near the fire. Gran was smoking her inevitable pipe. Granda was cleaning a salmon they had taken from the river soon before dark.

Both Cathy and Ewen looked to be asleep.

The day had started badly for them, with the fear of Mr. Crawford, and seeing the fight and the tent burned. He wished he could have spared them that. He wished that Dream Johnny could have stopped the croft being burned.

Dream Johnny and Dream Gran...

Had he, present day Johnny really been Dream Johnny? That was impossible. Maybe the fact that Dream Johnny and Dream Gran looked so like him and his real Gran was a trick of the eelreallys. But, somehow, he felt he had come back here specially. Or perhaps it was only that Dream Johnny and Dream Gran existed in his mind, in his dream, and had never ever been a living person. But that was impossible, too. There were too many coincidences. Dream Gran had been quite certain about him. And if she was only someone in his dream, why wasn't she identical to Real Gran? She had known him. As for Dream Johnny, he'd clearly seen Johnny as a different person from himself.

It was all very confusing. He sighed. He wondered if it could ever get sorted out in his mind. And what had happened after the croft had burned?

Had Dream Gran escaped from the fire? And what had happened to Dream Johnny and his family afterwards?

He fell asleep and dreamed...

...The croft blazed. Pieces of burning straw, caught in the up draught, swirling into a sky darkened by the black smoke.

"Gran!" he called again.

And then he saw her, though she had not been there moments before. She was sitting in the doorway as cool and still as a salmon pool. Her black bonnet and dark plaid shawl silhouetted her against the dark orange flames. She was smoking her pipe, calmly, serenely, as if it was the evening of a summer's day. Behind her, and it seemed around her, the flames roared. A huge chunk of roof fell with an enormous crash. Now there was no roof left.

Gran still sat as if she was unaware of the chaos round her.

"Gran!" Johnny called again. "Oh Gran!"

He couldn't understand how she was not herself burning. Flames all round, yet she untouched. It was impossible. Unless, of course, it wasn't Gran, but her eelreally.

And if it was that, she must already be dead.

The realisation screamed from his lips in a shout of despair and grief. "Graaaaaan!"

Behind him, the little ones were screaming too, but he guessed not because they understood like he.

And the terrible sadness and despair gripped his throat and squeezed until he could no longer shout Gran's name. It came out instead as a whisper hardly heard above the roar of the fire.

"Gran!"

And he knew he no longer wished to live himself. He wanted to die, too, and be with his wonderful Gran again. He leaped towards the house, only half knowing his intention.

He was stopped suddenly. A large hand grabbed his arm. "Don't be stupid, boy. The old fool chose that way. Go with your family."

"Let go! I swear you're the devil himself!"

Mr. Crawford chuckled. "I didn't kill her. She chose to die."

"You wicked man!" Johnny's voice wailed in grief. "Let go, let go!"

Mr. Crawford chuckled again. It was that which decided Johnny. Bad enough that he had had to watch Gran die. And at the hands of this evil devil. But for him to chuckle in amusement.

Johnny's hand felt to his belt. His hand closed over the handle of Granny's dirk. He didn't think what he was doing. He just wanted Mr. Crawford to understand that they could defend themselves. He pulled it out.

"Take that!" he cried. And stabbed. Not intending to hurt, not thinking that it would. Simply to show Mr. Crawford that he could fight back.

Mr. Crawford stopped chuckling. His face looked both shocked and puzzled, as if he hadn't expected that. There was no smile now. His hand went to his side where the knife had pierced between his ribs. He pulled at the handle.

For a moment, Johnny thought he was about to be stabbed himself by Mr. Crawford. But instead, the man threw the knife with such a power that it was as if he was trying to throw away the wound with it. It flew over the top of the rowan and towards the little river.

Then Mr. Crawford sighed. It was the sigh of a man who had done all he was ever going to do. He slumped to the floor and lay there staring up into the smoky sky. A trickle of blood oozed from his ribs and stained the white trousers.

"I didn't mean — I didn't..." Johnny began.

Then several hands grabbed him roughly. They twisted his arms behind him, despite mum's cries. They corded his arms so tight that his wrists hurt. An Reith picked him up and threw him over the saddle of one of the horses. The breath was squashed from him, and he lay with his head hung one side and his legs the other, like a sack of tatties.

An Reith mounted the horse, sitting behind the saddle with Johnny hanging in front. He clicked the horse to make it set off. The saddle dug into Johnny's stomach and the cord round his wrists was so tight that his hands felt numb. He guessed the blood was not reaching them properly.

"You're for the judge and the hangman's noose, my lad!" said An Reith. Johnny saw the man's red eyes and thought he recognized pleasure in them at his fearsome words. "Murder, plain and evil murder!"...

Chapter 14

...Johnny awoke from the dream and his stomach ached, as if he'd eaten something that had poisoned him. But he'd not eaten any of the mussels, so it couldn't be that.

He switched on his torch and pulled at the T shirt he wore for sleeping. The pain was awful, like he'd been lying on a lump. He groped against the straw but could find nothing there.

So it had to be the dream, he thought. Dream? That was a nightmare. The terrible events of the dream slipped into his mind. He remembered Dream Gran in the entrance to the burning croft, the fight with Mr. Crawford, the awful event with the knife. Then the men tying him and throwing him over the horse. He shuddered.

Johnny shone the torch at his wrist. The red rings were clear to see, as if it had happened to him, too.

Poor Dream Johnny, he thought. It was so unfair, and he hadn't really meant to hurt Mr. Crawford. Just as I wouldn't have. It was the unfairness of it all made it happen.

His stomach hurt less now, but his wrists still throbbed. I don't really understand this, he thought. How can I get hurt in a dream? Or is it really a dream? He looked round the tent. Everyone else was asleep. Yes, of course. It's a dream. That's all. But no, it's not just that. You don't get sore wrists and stomach ache dreaming. Somehow, in the dreams, I really become Dream Johnny. Which means... which means...

He remembered the cruel words of An Reith as they rode off. "You're for the judge and the hangman's noose, my lad! Murder, plain evil murder!"...

Johnny shuddered. It was terrible to think of what had happened afterwards to Dream Johnny. But if he fell asleep now and dreamed again, would he end up like Dream Johnny? He couldn't stop another shudder. Because if he did, as he now guessed, become Dream Johnny

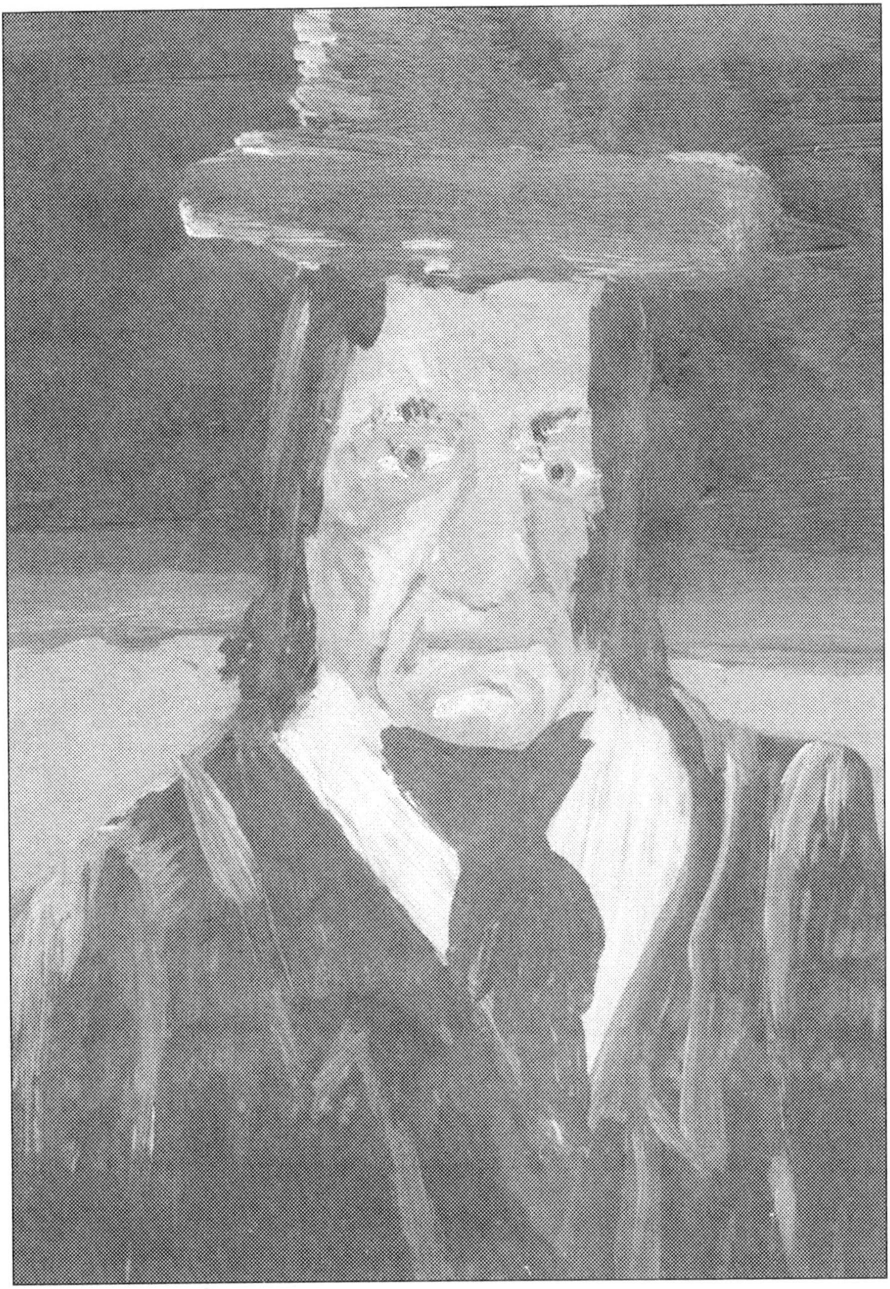

in his sleep, what would happen in the end? He propped himself up on one arm and wondered about reading something. He didn't want to go to sleep now, it seemed too risky. Better to stay awake and sleep in the daylight instead.

He looked at Ewen and Cathy, breathing deeply beside him. And Granda and Gran near the entrance. And next to them, Riley the dog, his nose pressed down on his paws.

And at that same moment, the dog's head shot up. It gave a yelp of joy, stood and lashed its tail.

Johnny knew. Outside the tent was the other Johnny. Waiting. Wanting to speak to him.

He gulped, and wondered if it was safe. If Dream Johnny had been hanged, maybe he'd want some sort of revenge like in one of those horror films. But this wasn't films. Real life didn't stop after a couple of hours of entertainment. And anyway, Dream Johnny understood about him, real Johnny, and obviously wanted him for something important. He'd said that in the rain and wind. He wanted Johnny to help him, and to search — yes, that was what he'd said,

"Seek also for me."

But what did that mean. Seek where? How? For the dream? For the ghost? For the bones of his dead ancestor?

Riley interrupted his thoughts. The dog danced up and down as if the Dream Johnny was right in front of him and speaking to the animal. Riley's yelps of joy became louder and louder.

Johnny decided. He would have to go outside and talk to Dream Johnny. He was almost sure he had nothing to fear. For, in some way, the ghost needed his help. He had to find out how.

And he guessed that the Eelreally ram wasn't there. He thought of the ram, as he seized the torch again and picked his way over Ewen and Cathy and past Granda and Gran. Those red eyes — both the ram and the nasty man in the dream — what was his name — yes, An Reith, that was it — had peculiar eyes. Could they be one and the same?

He didn't know.

Riley turned to look at him, as if to say, "At last, come on!"

It wasn't raining for once, but the night was cold and he guessed there was a light frost.

Dream Johnny stood beside the mound. He began speaking the

instant Johnny emerged from the bender, even before a joyful Riley could reach him. It was still difficult to understand what he said, though the wind had also gone, because there were several words in the old Gaelic which he did not understand.

" Ye've naething to fear from me... nae got long... nae a thing to fear... I am ye as ye are me... I cannae find nae rest... Great Sheep... ye will understand all... find my gran and find me... let us lie in the kirkyard togaither... An Reith watches always, seeking me again. Yet he cannae harm me in the kirkyard. D'ye ken?"

He understood enough. "Yes, I think so. But the dreams. They're getting worse. You — when that man they called An Reith, The Ram, took you. Did they hang you?"

"Nay, nay. Bide awhile. Gae ye ae sloom. Gae now, my ain Johnny."

"I didn't understand that bit. What's sloom? What do you mean?"

"Sleep again, young Johnny. Sleep so ye can understand everything. Then ye shall know what to do. Fear nothing. Old red An Reith seeks me, not ye. But we are alike, ye and me. For ye are my ain brother's gran'child's gran'child's gran'child. Now d'ye understand a wee bit more?"

"Yes I think so. But what is *your* name. Is it really the same as mine?"

The ghost chuckled. "Aye, aye, and did I not have a brother Ewen and a sister Cathy like ye? Aye! And a dog like yon, though we named him Cull. Nigh two hundred years I've waited ye, and I thank God ye're here now."

At the word Cull, Riley's ears pricked up and he gave a little yelp.

Then, suddenly, the eelreally's voice changed. "Aakhhh nae, nae, it cannae be time!" He pointed beyond Johnny.

Johnny didn't need to turn to know who — or what was there. An Reith. The red eyed ram. The evil man from the day the croft was burned down. But he turned even so.

The ram pawed the ground, some distance away down the shore, as if it meant to charge at any moment. Its great head bucked up and down as a warning that it would soon come.

"I must away. Fare ye well, my Johnny lad!"

Johnny turned back at Dream Johnny's words. "Help me as I have asked ye, my Johnny. Help my granmaither too. I must away, for An Reith will nae let me stay here long. Fare ye well, my bonny lad.

Farewell. I must away. And may God bless ye all."

Riley gave a single whine as if he had understood every word. "Goodbye!" real Johnny called. "Goodbye, eelreally Johnny."

The ghost waved and slowly disappeared. Johnny felt a tear in the corner of his eye. He brushed it angrily away, and turned to look at An Reith. But the ram had already disappeared.

He sighed. "There's only one thing to do. Go back to sleep. If I can. And find out what happens." He picked his way through the tent and lay down. "But getting to sleep after all this won't be easy."

That was the last thought. Then he was there again, back on the lumpy horse, smoke from the burning croft drifting towards him like beckoning fingers, making him cough.

Somewhere behind he heard his brother and sister wailing in terror, and his mum and dad pleading for mercy for him.

He lifted his head to breathe better and saw the croft.

Gran was standing in the doorway, calling him. "Come, Johnny, come to me. I will protect you. Come quickly. Slide off the horse."

He needed no second invitation. He bucked his body twice, and before An Reith could grab him, Johnny slid down the horse.

At the same moment he remembered the cords which bound him. Hadn't Gran realised? He couldn't run!

And remembered something else. Gran was dead in the fire!

His feet hit the pebbles of the shore and he tumbled over. Instantly, a shape lunged at him. It was Cull! Before he had time to speak to the dog or do anything, it had snatched with sharp teeth at the cord round his ankles, and tugged.

The cord parted instantly and his legs were free! He stood at the very moment that An Reith turned his horse to ride at him. Two other men dashed forward to grab at him, too, but Cull knew his duty.

He stood between Johnny and the two ruffians and bared his teeth. He wasn't a huge dog, but his teeth looked (and were) sharp as slashing knives. The men hesitated. Only for an instant, but enough. Before An Reith could reach him, he set off at a run up the beach.

Gran was still in the doorway and still beckoning. He reached her just as An Reith did the same. An Reith reached over the side of the horse and made a grab.

Gran seemed to rise in stature. "No!" she cried.

The horse shied, whether because it could see Gran's eelreally or because of the fire, Johnny didn't know. But An Reith's grab missed. He reached the door, passed beside — or was it through Gran? — and went in.

Outside, Cull howled.

Chapter 15

Standing in very the middle of the blazing building, Johnny turned to look back towards the entrance. Gran's ghost had seated herself again and was puffing at her pipe. She looked so calm, gazing out of the entrance to the croft as she so often did, looking towards the sea and the shore. breathing in the clear sea air.

But Johnny's air wasn't mackerel sky fresh. The heat round him was colossal and he couldn't stop himself coughing in the smoke. Glowing straw ash tumbled all round, like orange rain, burning his hands and face. He could hear An Reith and the other men outside, shouting something. But no-one tried to follow him in.

He was caught in a fit of terrible coughing. It bent him double and in bending he saw that there was less smoke near the floor.

He crouched down, using the flash of the flames to crawl over the earth floor towards the back of the room. He was no longer sure why he had gone back in, except Gran had beckoned him.

Gran. Yes, that *was* why he had returned. Because, though he knew she was dead because of the sigh of her eelreally seated in the cottage entrance, impervious to flame, he wanted to find her body. To give her a proper burial. If he could drag her out, it wouldn't matter any more when An Reith grabbed him. Aye, even boys of his age were hanged for much less than killing His Grace's manager, he reasoned. But if I have to die, at least Gran will be laid in a proper place. Even His Grace's men will not hold a corpse to account.

He coughed again as another cloud of smoke wafted down, filling his lungs and obscuring his vision. A chunk of burning thatch fell and hit his forehead. He knocked at it but it stuck there and burned into him before he at last managed to brush it aside. He could feel it had burned him badly.

Not that it mattered now. If he could just find Gran's body, she could be buried in the churchyard where she'd want to be, near her husband and other relatives.

The heat in the back of the croft was colossal and his head throbbed. But there was less smoke, because the dry heather beds had already burned out. Only one patch where a thin plume of smoke rose was still alight.

He saw instantly, just for a second, in a flickering of flame light, that Gran lay there, where the plume of smoke rose like a signal.

Reaching her, he tried to grasp her round the shoulders. Instantly, he felt pain and realised that she was lying beside smouldering wood and that it had burned his hands. He hardly bothered, the pain and the sense of too much heat in his forehead was greater.

He managed to half stand, ready to drag her body, but immediately his head was back in all the smoke. He had to let go, sink to the ground, and cough over and over.

As soon as the coughing eased, he crouched back near Gran. Now he felt pain from the hot ground in his knees. But before he could grasp her again, he heard a voice.

"Johnny MacPhee! Johnny MacPhee, do you hear me?"

"Aye," he half called and half coughed back.

"You know my voice. This is An Reith of the red eyes. The Ram. There is no escape for you. Come out, and be taken to the magistrate."

"Aye, aye, I hear ye," he managed to call back through the crackling and crunching of the fire. Then the smoke caught him again and he coughed into speechlessness.

"Then come out!" An Reith called. "Come out. Your Gran can go to the devil, you'll meet her there soon enough. Come out for justice to be done."

"My Gran!" he managed to call back. The smoke grew ever thicker low down in the room, and he coughed more and more. He gasped at the remaining air, and because it was polluted with the smoke, could not breathe properly and coughed even more.

He thought he heard Cull outside, alternately whining and yelping. And perhaps it was dad's voice pleading with him to come out. Not now, not now, he couldn't.

Grasping Gran round the armpits, he tried to drag her a last time, but his strength was failing.

He let her down as he coughed again and again.

"Johnny MacPhee!"

An Reith's voice was filled with anger.

"You cannot escape me! I will have you to justice. Do you understand? You will not escape me. If you will not come to me, I shall come to you and drag you from the house to the magistrates. You will not cheat death. I will not leave Aakkhamuir until I have you, or until we are both lying in the kirkyard. You hear me? You killed my friend Crawford. The Ram keeps his word. For ever and ever."

"You cannot hang me if I am already in a churchyard!" Johnny managed to splutter back, and thought to himself: <u>No evil can enter there. Not even An Reith.</u>

"But you are not in holy ground! This is a dirty tinker croft which scars the landscape and robs His Grace of his rightful money." An Reith's voice sounded closer now. Johnny peered towards the doorway. A huge white ram stood in it.

Even as Johnny began to believe the impossible evidence of his own eyes, the ram lowered its head, and charged through the smoke and flame towards him. Its feet seemed to slip on hot ash which wisped up and away through the now multi-holed roof.

The smoke was making Johnny feel very dizzy and it was difficult to think straight. Even so, a huge white ram charging through the little croft was impossible. But it was there, in front, about to smash into him. Or would it smash? No! He had somehow seen wrong. Maybe it was the smoke. But this wasn't a huge white ram at all. It was a man, not an animal. An Reith himself! An Reith, trying to snatch him from the ruins. The wicked man only nicknamed the ram. His red eyes glaring in anger.

As one of An Reith's hands grabbed at Johnny, the boy found enough energy to half roll, and half fall away from him. He crashed a shoulder into the side of the fireplace.

The loose fireplace stone, where they normally hid Gran's old dirk, toppled and fell. It missed Johnny but must have hit An Reith, for as he himself scrunched onto the ground, he heard the man cry in pain. At the same time, the last of the roof beams fell. Johnny glimpsed up and saw the huge wood gable beam, roaring with flame, falling towards his forehead.

The last thing he saw was Gran's face, smiling her deep love for her grandson through the haze.

His last thought was a wish, a prayer, to someone who might come after. Someone who must come. Whether it was his own brother or sister or their children or grandchildren. "Find my gran and find me... let us lie in the kirkyard togaither."

Chapter 16

Johnny awoke on another bright morning. He coughed for several moments before he remembered that he was back in real life. His aching wrists, and his head throbbing and burning were real enough. And his hands, too, ached as if there was no skin left.

It was a stupid thought, that anything *could* have happened to his hands. But then, his wrists had been sore from the ropes. Maybe his hands...

He pulled them out from under the blanket and stared at them. Even half expecting there to be something wrong, it still came as a shock. His hands had been perfectly normal the night before. Now they were covered in awful black and red blisters, as if they had been in the heart of a bad fire, and the pain was terrible.

"Gran!" he screamed in horror. But even as he looked, the injuries started to fade, and before Gran had time to tuck her head into the tent entrance, they had already gone. They were back to being ordinary, straightforward, hands with not a blemish on them. And so too had his wrists from the vicious red rings of being tied with the rope from when Dream Johnny's wrists were tied.

"What?" Gran shouted from the bender entrance, glaring at him. Then soothed, "Nightmare?"

"Yeah, something like that," he sighed. "It's OK though."

"Just as well." Gran disappeared from the tent entrance. He heard her chuntering as she walked off. "Some of us is busy people, some is. Some of us can't spend all our lives a-chasing eelreallys and staying in bed till all hours."

Gran's words brought him back to reality again like nothing else could. Life had to go on, had to be faced. Because it was Now, not Then. And he was back to being his normal safe. He knew he had left Dream Johnny behind in the dream.

Ewen and Cathy were already up, because he was the last person in the bender. Somehow, it seemed, he had awoken from a horror. Not just of the dream, or nightmare as it had become. But awoken out of the past and was now firmly in the present. No-one had said this to him, it was just something he *realised.*

He felt great relief, that he had come out of the dream and was normal. More or less. But in the front of his mind, even stronger than the events of the fire, and the deaths of Dream Johnny and An Reith, was a remembered phrase.

...Find my gran and find me... let us lie in the kirkyard togaither.

He stretched, reached for his clothes, and dressed before emerging into the sunshine.

Granda and Gran were seated by the fire cooking breakfast.

"I dreamed again," said Johnny sipping a mug of tea which Granda had made.

"Aye, you made that plain enough," said Gran, flicking strips of sizzling bacon over in the frying pan so that the fat splattered into the flames, making them chatter with rage.

Johnny told them the details of the dream, adding, "I understand now, about when Dream Gran said not to make the same mistake again. In the dream, I stabbed Mr. Crawford. They took me away to hang. But I escaped and died when the croft burned. He did, I mean."

He felt free to say such scary things as Ewen and Cathy were down the shore, throwing stones at a bobbing piece of driftwood.

"Aye, you were right second time," Gran nodded. "Not you, your eelreally. My eelreally. Mr. Crawford's eelreally. And you didn't make the mistake again. It was a warning, no more, about what could happen. That's what eelreallies does. Isn't that what I said?"

"Only because you took the old dirk from me. I wonder where it is now?"

She shrugged. "I threw it. Towards yonder burn. It's best there, where it come from."

"I'm glad. I wouldn't want it any more."

Gran smiled and topped up his tea mug.

"What about Dream Gran's body?" Johnny asked. "She wanted to be given a proper burial. And I want to find Johnny's. An Reith's, I suppose, as well, though I doubt if he deserves it.

"AAakhh but he does. No-one wants to wander round like a great ram. His eelreally's trapped like our own people's are. The man made mistakes. It was two centuries past. So did lots of others. We all does still. And it don't give no cause for not forgiving folk. So that don't give no cause for not doing the right thing by him."

Granda nodded. "Herr Breitmann's sending some men. I saw him earlier on. They're going to dig. There's an expert coming, an archaeologist, to help. If these people's under that mound, I ken they'll find them."

In the afternoon, Land Rovers disgorged eight people. They were armed with spades, and there was a smiling archaeologist, as Herr Breitmann had promised — a short, wiry man.

"You kids can help," the archaeologist, Dr. Swift announced, as his helpers set up posh modern tents a few yards away from the mound.

"Even Ewen?" Johnny asked incredulously.

Dr. Swift ran a hand through his short red beard. "I don't see why not. He can help to carry things away."

By teatime, the men had cut away the turf which had spread over the remains, and the tops of blackened stones stared out into the dusk. Ewen had soon given up, but Johnny and Cathy had worked the whole afternoon, carrying away tumps of turf and bringing the men and women frequent mugs of Granda's smoke tainted tea.

In the evening, Granda treated all the visitors to mackerel steaks garnished with raspberry vinegar and surrounded by fresh salad and boiled tatties, as Gran insisted on calling them.

As they ate, Johnny explained about the dreams and the eelreallys. He felt almost as if the ghosts of those poor people were seated by the fire, too, listening and agreeing with what he said. Even An Reith.

Almost in answer, Dr. Swift told them what had happened to the people who had been cleared from the land by the Great Sheep.

It had been a time of terrible sorrow and suffering. Some had been sent to Canada, often without any clothes other than those they stood up in. There, many were just dumped on the shores and left in all weathers, even having to build their own homes and sleep in the open until they did.

Others moved to the Scottish coasts and became fishermen. Still more drifted to the towns and cities, especially Glasgow. And some became travelling people, like the MacPhees.

"They were terrible times," he concluded. "And all so the landowners could keep sheep and make money. And that's why there are huge chunks of Scotland where almost no-one lives today."

The following morning, after Johnny had slept a dreamless night, and after a good breakfast of more of Granda's fire smoked bacon with thick wedges of bread wrapped round, the archaeologists resumed their work.

Johnny watched as the men dug all the rest of that day, sifting every bit of soil for tiny artifacts from the ruins of the little croft house known as Aakkhamuir. Johnny and Cathy helped hold sieves as they checked every speck of soil. They carried away buckets of checked soil, too, and poured them onto a growing heap. Ewen 'helped' by clambering up the heap every few minutes and trampling it down, until Dr. Swift told him off and Granda shouted.

Much of the mound was caused by the old gable walls of the cottage which had crashed in when the croft burned. They were blackened with ancient soot. There were bits of charred wood, too, so old that it was difficult to tell which was soil and which timber.

Here and there, the searchers found little chunks of broken pottery, part of a halter for a cow, old hooks, rust ridden tools, traces of cloth, and the remains of an old copper kettle and an iron pot. They set up a trestle table, and lay the items out.

Here sat one of the archaeologists, who gave every item a special code number and put each into a small transparent bag. Only then would they let the children examine the finds.

But there were few more. A thin buckle from a belt, a metal button, a broken metal pin, an old copper coin, part of a stool.

Again that night, Johnny had no dreams.

The next day, as they reached the original level of the floor, Johnny watched their every action instead of helping.

And towards that evening, they found a skeleton. It was exactly where Johnny had expected her to be — in the remains of the time preserved bracken bedding at the back of the house.

Dr. Swift called Johnny and Cathy over. "There," he said, wafting specks of soil off amber coloured bones. "The one you call Dream Gran, unless I'm much mistaken."

Carefully, reverentially, Dr. Swift and his team took out the bones of Dream Gran. They placed them in larger plastic bags.

Johnny gazed at the skull of Dream Gran. It wasn't in the least scary, even though Cathy insisted on going "Eugh!" every few moments. Johnny imagined her face, as he had seen it in the dreams, still smiling kindly at him. And after all, he knew he was doing what the dream people wanted.

Next morning, they quickly found a second skeleton. And this time, Johnny knew instantly it was his own Dream person's.

"This should be your job," said Dr. Swift. Johnny squatted beside the famous archaeologist in the ruins and look down at the skull which others were slowly clearing of soil in order to lift it out safely. Dr. Swift showed Johnny how to loosen the soil with the very tip of a trowel, and then dust it away with an extremely soft paint brush.

So Johnny reverentially lifted each of the dry sand coloured bones of his dead dream self out of the ground and passed them to a nearby archaeologist to place in the bags. As his hands closed on the sides of the skull, he felt a tear run down his cheek and drip onto the ground.

<u>Hello at last</u>, he thought.

Later that morning, the diggers lifted a large stone and underneath found a third skeleton. "This must be An Reith," said Dr. Swift. They treated his remains exactly as they had the others, with gentleness and respect.

Then everything they found was sent away in one of the Land Rovers to have them all checked by experts, to discover things about the people of two hundred years before — how small they were, how they lived.

But not how or what they thought, because that wasn't possible. And anyway, as Johnny said, "I know that already. I saw them and they talked to me. And I will be back to complete the rest of the promise, when the bones come back from the experts," he added.

Soon after all the interesting contents of the mound had been removed, the archaeologists — helped by Johnny, Cathy and a more than usually enthusiastic Ewen, put the soil and rocks back into the mound. They covered it over with the turf they'd cut off at first.

The following day, everyone helped to take down the old bender and to pack everything onto the handcart. The archaeologists left in their Land Rovers to return to their university.

And Johnny and his family set off, too. This time, they pushed the cart round the side of the mound, but when they reached the next, it was "One last heave" according to Granda to get over it. Just like when they came. And so the holiday ended.

But not quite.

Chapter 17

Summer had gone, and the first leaves were tumbling from the trees.

Squashed between Granda and Gran's in Granda's old battered transit van, Johnny felt warm and safe.

The van picked its way along narrow lanes to the village nearest to the old mound. Granda parked on the grass verge outside one of the small stone cottages.

"Done it and half an hour to spare," Granda announced, climbing out of the van. "And I reckon that's them waiting in the kirkyard this very minute and early theirselves," he announced.

Funeral or no, Gran insisted on getting her foul blackened pipe going.

<u>Well,</u> Johnny thought, <u>We might all choke to death, but so will, the midges.</u> He swiped at few, but it did no good. Within seconds, a huge cloud had settled round his head and round Granda's. As he expected, they kept well clear of Gran.

Granda set off towards the churchyard. At the entrance, a huge old rowan tree dipped its arching branches, and the summer's red berries lay showered on the ground.

Six people — two of them grave diggers — awaited them in the kirkyard. Two were Dr. Swift and another archaeologist. A third, Herr Breitmann, in a smart business suit, held a bundle of cloth under his arm, though Johnny didn't get chance to ask what it contained. The fourth person was a priest. Two holes, in different parts of the churchyard, had already been dug. And there were three coffins.

They lowered Dream Gran's coffin first. Johnny held one of the ropes, and was surprised at how heavy it felt. Almost as if there was a person in there, and not just a few ochred bones.

Next, Dream Johnny's coffin was lowered in on top of his grandmother's. As he helped, Johnny thought of his dream relation and was thankful that he was doing what he knew the eelreally wanted.

Johnny wondered about putting something into the grave. Just as a token of love. He thought of the golden half guinea, but Herr Breitmann had already offered to buy it after it had been properly valued. He wondered whether he ought to have brought the dirk back from the river, and put that in, for that had, after all, belonged to Gran and Johnny. But when he thought of how the knife had been last used, he realised it wasn't suitable.

And then his eyes glimpsed the huge old rowan at the entrance to the kirkyard. It felt like an omen. There had been just such a tree beside the old croft before it was burned.

Before the first spade of soil could be thrown on top of Dream Johnny's coffin, Johnny said, softly, "Wait, there's something I must do."

He walked back top the entrance, reached up, and plucked a twig of rowan, heavy with red berries, from the old tree. He carried it back, and dropped it on top of Dream Johnny's coffin. Then everyone in the party threw on a handful of the soil, before the gravediggers finished filling it in.

The ritual was repeated at the second hole, some distance from the first. An Reith's grave. And once again, Johnny dropped a twig of rowan onto it.

When both holes had been filled in, and the small party had finished their prayers and their farewells, Mr. Breitmann unwrapped the strange cloth parcel. In it, were two large brass plaques which he had paid for.

Johnny placed the first on top of the soil where Dream Gran and Dream Johnny's bones lay. The brass plaque read,

> *Here lie Granny MacPhee, an elderly woman, and Johnny MacPhee, a boy of about 11 years, victims at the croft Aakkhamuir of the Highland Clearances (The Great Sheep), Autumn 1785. Rest now in peace.*

There was a similar plaque for An Reith. His read,

> *Here lies the body of a man for whom only a nickname, An Reith (The Ram) is known. A victim of the Highland Clearances (The Great Sheep), Autumn 1785. Rest now in peace.*

Johnny felt a tear run down his cheek. It wasn't especially one of sorrow, but of pity for the three victims of those evil times.

Herr Breitmann tapped him on the arm and interrupted his musings. "Come on, I have cakes and your favourite *salmon* sandwiches ready for us at my home."

Afterwards, Granda announced: "Come on, you great noodles, we cannae leave here without taking a wee stroll along the beach to the old croft of Aakkhamuir. Come."

The walk seemed much shorter without a loaded cart to push. And it looked much as they had left it. On top, a sheep grazed casually. Nearby were several more.

Johnny picked up a flat stone from the shore and skimmed it over the sea. Near him, Gran and Granda linked arms and gazed out to sea.

"Aye, they were days right enough," Granda sighed.

"Days of evil and terror," Gran nodded.

Johnny skimmed another stone towards the place they had pegged out the muscles on that first night.

<u>But we have done what the eelreallys wanted</u>, Johnny thought. <u>May they rest now in peace, knowing we have done that, and given them the rest they wanted.</u>

"Aakhh! We'd best be off," Granda said. "Afore dark."

"Aye," Gran agreed, "This may have been home once for our people, but nae now. With no bender, the night's be chill as a fishy finger."

"As the gaze of red-eyed An Reith," Johnny whispered to himself.

He turned for a last look along the beach before they left. The sheep at the croft had gone, but nearby, two sheep grazed on the salt-bleached grass at the top of the shore.

And then, as if an answer to what he had said about the eyes of An Reith, there was a third. Standing, in the shallows of the sea, ripples dancing round its ankles. A huge white ram. It turned its head towards him. Though too far off to see its look clearly, Johnny no longer felt scared. Instead, it was like something from the past. Something gone.

The huge ram nodded its head slowly up and down at Johnny. It looked as if it agreed, and was glad of what he had done. And into Johnny's mind came thoughts from the ram, as they had before, on the day he had first seen it.

"You have done well. Thank you. It is over now, at last. The past has gone for ever and we are at peace."

The eyes still shone red, but they no longer looked angry. It shook its head at him. Up and down. Once, twice. Then the ram turned away and walked steadily up the shore and between the two sheep.

And vanished.

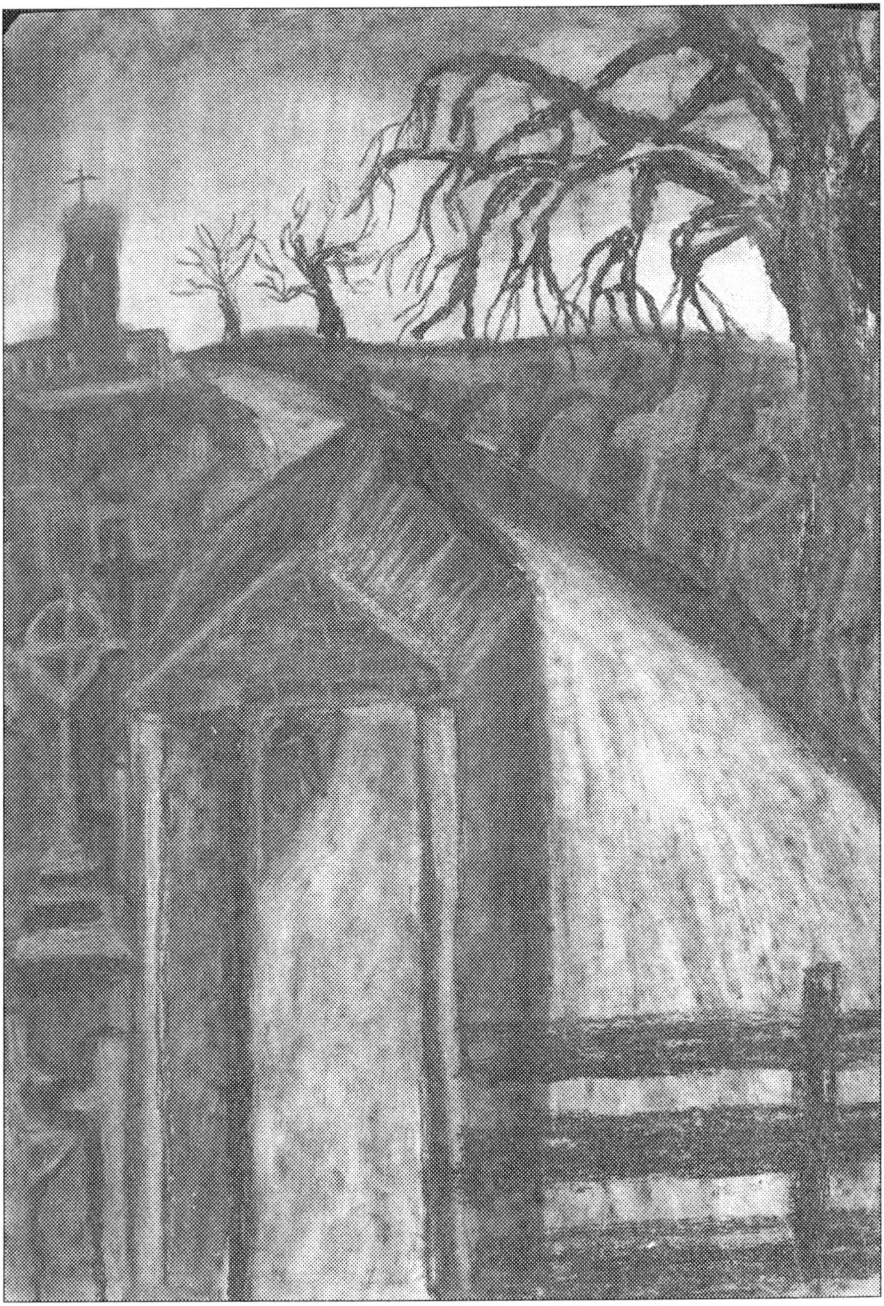